BKM
CS

Jost

☑ **P9-BZN-219**

AN — MMP
MCM
1 SB

X

Also available in Large Print
by Simon Brett:

Murder Unprompted
Not Dead, Only Resting

Dead Romantic

Simon Brett

G.K.HALL &CO.
Boston, Massachusetts
1986

To Halcy

Published in Large Print by arrangement with
Charles Scribner's Sons.

The poem by Emily Dickinson comes from *The Poems of
Emily Dickinson* edited by Thomas H. Johnson,
Cambridge, Mass., and the Belknap Press of Harvard
University Press.

G.K. Hall Large Print Book Series.

Set in 16 pt. Plantin.

Library of Congress Cataloging in Publication Data

Brett, Simon.
  Dead Romantic.

  1. Large type books.   I. Title.
[PR6052.R4296D39 1986b]   823'.914   86-14271
ISBN 0-8161-4135-5 (lg. print)

PART ONE

The Murder

1

There was no telephone at the cottage, so Mrs Rankin had to drive three miles before she could inform the police of the murder. The concentration required by driving had calmed her a little, but her hands were still shaking so much that she misdialled three times before she got through on the 999 call.

When asked which service she required, she was surprised how steady her voice sounded as she replied, 'Police.'

She didn't use the word 'murder'. She just said that she had found a dead body in the bedroom of Winter Jasmine Cottage.

Prompted by the impassive voice at the other end of the phone, she identified herself as Beryl Margaret Rankin, of 43, Thorley Drive, Shorton, West Sussex. No, she was not the owner of Winter Jasmine Cottage. The property was owned by Mrs

Ivy Waterstone, who lived in Kensington. She gave the address and phone number. No, Mrs Waterstone was rarely at the cottage. Most of the time it was let out, by the week or fortnight, to holiday-makers. It was Mrs Rankin's job to move in between lets, clean up and check the inventory of contents.

The name of that weekend's tenant was Mr Edward Farrar. No, she hadn't met him. No, she didn't have an address for him. She was sure Mrs Waterstone would, though.

Was the cottage open? Oh dear, yes. She had been in such a state when she rushed out that she had not thought to lock the door.

Yes, if the police insisted, she would go back to the cottage and wait for them. But she would wait outside.

They would be there within twenty minutes.

'Fine,' she said. 'See you then.'

The incongruity of that final chattiness hit Mrs Rankin as she walked away from the phone-box, and a gasp like hysterical laughter almost winded her. When breath returned, she was trembling uncontrollably. She opened the car door on her fourth attempt and, shivering in her seat, tried to collect herself sufficiently to drive back.

But the image she had forced out of her mind returned with reinforced clarity. She was not an imaginative woman, but she did not need imagination. She had seen the reality too recently.

She closed her eyes, but that only seemed to make the picture more vivid. The sour, animal smell was in her nostrils, and she could see the tangle of sheets, crisp new sheets with the neat lines of their packaged folds still showing and their regular design of green and brown sprigs on a beige background disrupted by random smears of brown blood. She could also see the naked body, unseamed by a long frontal slash, whose edges of drained flesh gaped to show a glimpse of discoloured bone. It no longer had any human characteristics; it was like a carcass hooked up on a butcher's rail. But that did not make it any less shocking.

She could also see, too vividly, the new nightdress that lay beside the bed, its crisp white linen crumpled and its pleated front stiff with dried blood.

It was a quarter of an hour before she had stopped shaking sufficiently to turn the key in the ignition. She drove badly, twitching at corners, starting at the whiteness of the lines on the road. And the only thought that could move the body from the centre of her mind was of her job, the cleaning of Winter Jasmine Cottage. That thought steadied her a little, rationalised the death, made it part of normal life.

She didn't think any blood had gone on to the carpet. The sheets obviously would have to be destroyed, surely even the much-advertised biological washing powders wouldn't shift that lot. But then the sheets didn't belong to the cottage; it was one of the conditions of the rental that the tenants should bring their own; so that wasn't her problem. Still, the wooden headboard of the bed would have to be swabbed down and polished. And maybe there had been a few splashes on the wallpaper. That might wash off—would wash off if it was a vinyl wall paper like Mr Rankin had just put up in their kitchen. But she didn't think it probable that it was vinyl in the bedroom of Winter Jasmine Cottage. Then of course there was the mattress. . . . With that amount of blood, some must have seeped through into the mattress. It might wash

out, or maybe it could be steam-cleaned.
. . . At worst it could just be turned over.
But that wouldn't really *do* . . . other tenants might turn it back . . . you never knew
what the tenants were going to get up to
when they were alone in the place. . . .

Obsessive concentration on such details
got Mrs Rankin back to the cottage in relative safety. As she turned into the drive, she
saw blue light from a police car flashing
intermittently on the shiny leaves of the high
laurel hedge. They had got there before her.

In fact, by the time she had brought her
car to an untidy, jerky stop beside a brown
Austin Maxi, the police had already looked
at the body in the bedroom. They had
looked at the blood-stained, black-handled
sheath-knife that lay on the floor beside the
bed.

And, though they did not know the details of the clash of two virginities which
had led to the crime, the police were in no
doubt that they were dealing with a case of
murder.

PART TWO

Before The Murder

2

Madeleine Severn rang the bell again. Really, it would be a bit much if Aggie was out. Madeleine had often said that her sister should give her a key because she was round there so often, but Aggie had always resisted the suggestion. In Madeleine's view, this resistance probably came from her new brother-in-law rather than from her sister. Keith still seemed insecure about the two-year-old marriage and would no doubt regard Madeleine's having a key as some obscure assault on his masculinity.

She knew she was earlier than she had said, but her class had been cancelled. Her pupil, an eighteen-year-old Iranian who was being crammed for A-level English, had apparently developed mumps. Madeleine did not believe that missing a few classes would make much difference to the outcome of his examinations. He had hardly mastered the rudiments of the English language, let alone the refinements of its literature. Still, she felt appropriate mild sympathy for the mumps. Could be nasty for men, she knew. And have long-term effects.

She thought she heard a vague movement from upstairs and rang the bell again. She turned her back to the door and looked down through the jumble of roofs and television aerials to the grey October sea. It always depressed her slightly, this part of Brighton. Seemed to have all the disadvantages of the suburbs with none of the compensations of the town. Always made her feel glad of her own neat little house a few miles away in Kemp Town.

Unconsciously, Madeleine ran her hands down the sides of her peat-coloured overcoat, from the line of her brassière over the indentation of her waist to the soft swell of her hips. It was a characteristic gesture, an expression of well-being. And it was rarely that Madeleine Severn did not experience a feeling of well-being.

The skin that glowed through the wool under her hands was, she knew, smooth and unblemished. Unconsciously, her right hand moved up to feel the softness of her cheek. The seaside air gave her face a rosiness that stayed all the year round and, though spider-lines now gathered round the eyes and marked the creases from her nose to the corner of her lips, she was confident that she looked younger than her thirty-seven years. Her eyes, which John Kaczmarek had described all those years ago as 'forget-me-not wedded to violet', still sparkled, their colour seemingly intensified by her recent adoption of contact lenses. And the red-gold hair remained her chief glory. Though a few individual white strands sprayed out from the parting, these seemed only to set in relief the brightness of the rest. That day she wore it up. It was a working day and her hair showed her to be a working woman. It had been artlessly whipped into an untidy roll at the back, slackly pinioned by a slide of dark wood and leather.

The door behind her opened, and Madeleine turned to look at her sister. As ever she felt an access of pity. Though three years younger, there was no question that Aggie had worn less well. She had started with less natural advantages, and the events of the last twenty years had not enhanced those she did possess. Her black hair was lank, the skin beneath her mouth ragged with the traces of spots. Her customary pallor was at that moment gone, but not to rosiness, more to a kind of flush. And the depredations of childbearing on her figure were accentuated by the dressing-gown pulled loosely around her.

Madeleine raised an eyebrow. 'Just got up?'

'I thought you said you wouldn't be here till six.'

'A class got cancelled. Aren't I welcome?'

'Of course.' Aggie drew back untidily to let her sister into the hall. Then, in response to Madeleine's continuing quizzical expression, she mumbled, 'I was just, er, having a bath.'

Madeleine moved through into the cramped sitting room, as ever inwardly wincing at the dralon three-piece suite and the veneered oval coffee table. 'I thought you were a late-night bather.'

'Yes. Ideally. Matter of when I can fit it in, really.' Aggie hovered uneasily in the doorway.

'Don't let me stop you if you want to get dressed.'

'Yes, I'll. . . . Well, I'll make some tea first. Would you like a cup of tea?'

'Heaven.' Madeleine flopped on to the dralon settee. As ever, she was surprised at how comfortable it was. It just *looked* awful. Keith's taste, she felt sure. Left to her own devices, Aggie did not have a bad eye for design. But she was always so influenced by her various men. Subordinated her own tastes to theirs, even when, like Keith's, it was disastrous.

Aggie was visible through the hatch, filling the kettle at the kitchen sink. Madeleine pitched her voice up. 'When'll Laura be in?'

'Oh, she's not coming,' Aggie called back.

'Not coming? Why?'

'Some new boyfriend. Terry. She's going out for a meal with him.'

Madeleine was piqued. She felt a proprietorial interest in her sister's eldest child. Laura had been Aggie's first major mistake, an unwanted pregnancy at the age of seventeen by a married man who subsequently emigrated and never saw his daughter. Madeleine felt that she had helped her sister and parents through that crisis. She had given Aggie a lot of time during the pregnancy and then, when the baby was born, had been a more than dutiful aunt. Even during her last year at Oxford, when heavily under stress from approaching exams, she had made a point of going to her parents' home most weekends to help with Laura. And, as the child grew older, she had always been there, a sympathetic aunt—no, more a friend, she liked to think—the fixed emotional point that Aggie's own erratic life could not provide for her daughter. Madeleine and Laura had always been very close—closer, it was generally recognised, than Aggie and Laura. Until recently. Recently Laura had become less dependent on her aunt's advice, less interested in her aunt's opinions. Madeleine found it mildly hurtful. She knew that children must grow up to independence. She could project herself very effectively into the maternal role and understand the inevitable pangs caused by the weaning away of their young. She just wished Laura would realise that she, Madeleine, was not a mother, and that the girl could still benefit a great deal from her aunt's knowledge of the world.

But the hurt was only mild. Madeleine was confident; she knew that Laura would come back to her and that their unique bond would be restored.

'Ah. Madeleine. Hello.'

She was surprised to see Keith standing in the doorway. She had not heard the front door. He must have come from upstairs.

'Keith. I didn't know you were here.'

'No. I. . . . Well, got home from work early.'

As always, Madeleine was struck by the unattractiveness of his voice, its slack South Coast vowels. And again by his very ordinariness. He was not particularly good-looking. Tall, stooped in the doorway, his thinning hair ruffled as if he had just got up. He wore a grubby T-shirt and jeans, his working clothes. He was a plasterer by trade, and his large hands were permanently cracked and scored with engrained dust.

As always, Madeleine tried to smother her reaction to him, smother the feeling that Aggie had married so far beneath herself, that she had taken irreversible steps over some Rubicon of class. Aggie had perhaps not been in much of a position to make choices. With the stigma of Laura and the two children of her failed first marriage, perhaps she should have been grateful to find anyone willing to take on such a full family package. And Aggie herself never complained, never seemed struck by the incongruity of her situation, by the disparity between her education and that of her husband. Maybe, in some way Madeleine could not understand, Keith made Aggie happy.

'Came home and found your wife in the bath,' said Madeleine, with a little giggle.

'Er, yes.' Keith flushed, and turned abruptly away towards the kitchen. 'You making tea, sweetie?'

Madeleine winced at the endearment.

Aggie confirmed, unnecessarily, that she was indeed making tea. Keith hovered in the hall, uncertain where to go.

'Do come in and sit down,' said Madeleine.

Awkwardly, as if he were not in his own house, Keith obeyed. He flashed a brief, meaningless smile at his sister-in-law, but said nothing. He was not a talker, Keith. It was always Madeleine who had to make the effort to get any sort of conversation started.

'How's work?'

'Oh, you know. All right. Doing a new block of flats down Lancing.'

'Ah yes.' The conversation swirled in an eddy. Madeleine always had difficulty in finding follow-up questions on the subject of plastering. She had tried in the past, but found the attractions and satisfactions of the job so alien to her that she never got far. She also got the impression that Keith had no particular desire to talk about his work, anyway, which made her efforts a little dispiriting.

Fortunately, before Madeleine forced herself into some redundant enquiry about the merits of plasterboard, Aggie came in from the kitchen with a tray of tea. She poured it in silence, knowing well the milk and sugar requirements of the other two. Madeleine took a sip and, as ever, tried not to recoil at the taste. Keith liked his tea Indian and strong, and so that was how tea was always made in his household. 'Workman's tea.' Madeleine could not stop the phrase from forming in her mind.

Aggie did not sit down with her cup. 'I'd better go upstairs and get dressed after my, er, bath.'

As she spoke, she flashed a smile, almost a wink, at her husband, and Keith's lips seemed to twitch. Madeleine did not enquire; she was uninterested in their private jokes.

She made a couple more valiant efforts at conversation with Keith, but the feedback she received was so minimal that soon silence had reasserted itself. After a couple of minutes of this, Keith drained his cup noisily and rose to his full height. 'Snooker tonight. Got to check out my gear.'

And he went out through the kitchen to the shed in the back garden.

Madeleine lay back on the sofa and stretched out her toes. She felt tired, but it was a warm, cosy tiredness. There was something warm and cosy in her mind too, a glow of thought that every now and then flared into a little jet of excitement.

Aggie had cooked goulash. She had two completely different styles of cooking, the traditional English meat and two veg. that Keith favoured, and a more interesting repertoire that came from her home background and her more middle-class former marriage. Apparently without strain or awareness of any incongruity, she would switch from one to the other according to her company. Because Madeleine was there on her own, Aggie had cooked goulash. Had Keith also been present, they would all have eaten chops with mashed potatoes, carrots and peas.

As Madeleine had this thought, she realised how rarely she and Keith actually *were* there together for a meal. Whenever she was round, he seemed to be off somewhere . . . snooker, darts, the pub. It was an arrangement that suited her well, but for the first time she wondered whether he deliberately avoided her. This raised the question of Keith and Aggie talking about her together, actually discussing her. She did not like the idea and put it from her mind. Some things she preferred not to think about.

She watched Aggie as her sister cleared the plates and went out to the kitchen. Again the pity welled up. Life seemed to have dealt Aggie such a lousy hand: first, her unexceptional looks; then, the illegitimate daughter; continuing problems with unsuitable men. Even the pregnancies, the fruits of her relationships, had not been trouble-free. A baby lost at four months; an incompetent cervix, the doctors had said. And the two children of her former marriage only born after seven months of lying on her back (during the second of which periods Aggie's first husband had found

21

time for a new distraction, a dental nurse, for whom he left her). Aggie's seemed to be a history of gynaecological disaster. She had even reacted badly to the pill, and been taken off it after an alarming rise in blood pressure.

As ever, by comparison, Madeleine felt herself privileged. She also felt something else, an emotion she did not choose to define, but which in her rare moments of introspection threatened to be identified as glee.

As ever, when this cycle of thought started, it climaxed in pity for the fact that Aggie had never known real love, love that worked.

At least Madeleine had had that.

'Any dishy students in this new lot?' asked the object of her pity, entering with the fruit-bowl.

Madeleine tinkled a laugh. 'Certainly not the Iranian with mumps. He has a five o'clock shadow the minute after he's shaved. A distinctly prickly prospect.'

'Others?'

'There's a rather sweet boy who's just started with me. Got disastrous grades in his A-levels at Sixth Form College in the summer. Mother desperate for him to get to university—and, since his grades aren't good enough for anywhere else, she's set her sights on Oxford, of all places. Seems to think I can pull the famous trick yet again.' Madeleine sighed at the extravagance of such expectations, yet there was no humility in the sigh.

'And do you think you can?'

'Have to see. He's certainly not stupid. Whether he could carry off the interview, I don't know. Very nervous. You know, that coltish jumpiness of adolescence.'

'Name?'

'Grigson. Paul Grigson.'

'No doubt already got a crush on you.'

Another tinkly laugh. 'Oh, I don't know.'

But she did not deny the possibility. It didn't seem important whether or not an eighteen-year-old dreamt of her. But there was something else in her life, something new, that could, perhaps, be very important.

She damped down the thought, and let out a dramatic sigh. 'It's John's birthday today.'

Aggie looked properly solemn at the reference.

'He would have been thirty-nine.'

'So how long is it. . . ?'

'Nineteen years. Nineteen years and three weeks since he died.'

Aggie was respectfully silent, as she always was when John Kaczmarek was mentioned. It was as if she knew that nothing she might say could compete with her sister's memory, Madeleine's experience of real love, of love that had worked. But for John's premature death from leukaemia, no doubt Madeleine too would be married, Madeleine too would have children of her own.

The older sister looked up to see that Aggie was yawning.

'Sorry, Maddy. It's been terribly busy in the surgery this week. Some sort of virus going round. Everyone seems to have been in.' Aggie worked part-time as a receptionist for a local group practice. The money was not good and, for someone as conscientious as Aggie, the hours tended to escalate.

'Yes, I've had a busy week too,' said Madeleine. 'The trouble is, however much one tries not to, one does find oneself empathising with one's students, going through it all with them. The Jean Brodie syndrome, I suppose.'

24

'Sorry?'

'Living through one's students. Like Jean Brodie. As in *The Pride of*... Muriel Spark.'

Aggie shook her head. Of course, she had never read much. And, since she had been married to Keith, hardly at all. Madeleine noticed again that there were no books to be seen in the small sitting-room.

'Oh, never mind,' she said.

Just before she left, Madeleine went upstairs to the bathroom. Floating in the lavatory bowl, with a knot neatly tied in it, was a pink condom.

She flushed it away before sitting down, and put it from her mind. Some things she preferred not to think about.

Back in her Kemp Town house, Madeleine had a protracted bath. She washed her hair and lay back so that the long tendrils lay tickling on her shoulders. Their redness rippled with the water and she found herself thinking of the death of Ophelia. Gertrude's report of the suicide from *Hamlet* came into her mind. The poetry, like the bath-water, gave her a warm feeling. She looked up at the stripped pine shelves from which a profusion of pot-plants dangled. As she half-closed her unlensed eyes, the plants looked satisfyingly like a willow growing aslant a brook.

And the thought of death brought to life the other thought she had been nursing all day, the warm thought of a new love.

The electric blanket had warmed her single bed and she slipped blissfully under the duvet. She drowsed, and the warm thought of love was still with her.

Her hand slipped unconsciously to the greater warmth beneath her nightdress as she dreamed of the day when she would shed the pampered burden of her virginity.

3

Bernard Hopkins was lucky to find a vacant meter a hundred yards away and he parked his five-year-old brown Austin Maxi there. The drive from his house in Henfield had not taken long; he was lucky to be able to come in after the rush-hour. Anyone who watched him getting out of the car would have seen a tall man with an air of privacy about him. His dark brown eyes looked thoughtful, even pained. His brown hair had given in to grey at the temples, but the effect was not unattractive.

As he strode up the steep incline towards the school, he felt the stiff breeze from the sea behind him, but it was not cold. Definitely autumnal, but one of those glowing, hopeful autumnal days. He felt a little bubble of optimism rising in him. This time it was going to work. This time he could put past failures firmly behind him; this time it would be all right.

The white portico of the school had been overpainted many times as the salt air flaked off successive layers, and now it had the thick, blurred outline of cake icing. The railings to either side had also been painted many times, but not recently enough; from their feet, through cracked black paint, rust bled its stains onto the stone. The large door, with impressive brass knocker and letter-box, had also been painted too long ago. The white paint was greyish and, since the door was left on the latch all day, there was a patch worn bare by a long trail of students pushing their uninterested way inside.

At the side of the door a brass plate, giving an old-fashioned, dependable image like that of a country solicitor, bore the legend: 'GARRETTWAY SCHOOL OF LANGUAGES. Principal: J.P.G. GARRETT, M.A.'

Eschewing the worn patch on the door, Bernard Hopkins put his hand on the brass door-handle and walked inside.

The hall had once been magnificent, but now its proportions were destroyed by the new walls which cut randomly through the fine cornices and bosses of the ceiling. The walls were painted institutional grey, marginally relieved by the darker grey on the flat boarded doors which fire regulations had demanded.

The balance of the fine staircase up to the first floor had been upset by encroaching partitions and the one feature left untouched by 'improvement', the floor of black and white tiles, looked sadly diminished in this setting, like a monochrome television testcard.

A couple of chipboard notice-boards by the front door were dotted with cards offering accommodation, coloured sheets advertising discotheques, plays, Indian takeaways and minicabs. But there were not many. Nor was there any evidence of students, except for one abandoned file lying on a table. It was one of the school's slack periods; the busy time would come in the summer.

In each of the fire-officer-approved doors was an eye-level window of wired glass, but through only one of the four did light shine. Bernard could not resist moving along the wall to peer into the classroom.

The room was what the Garrettway brochure described as 'one of our ultra-modern language laboratories, equipped with all of the latest electronic technology'. But Bernard did not see the person he hoped for behind the tutorial desk. Instead, there sat a grubby young man of about thirty, a member of the staff to whom Bernard had not yet been introduced. The young man was engaged in an exhaustive picking of his nose, eyes fixed on some abstract point in the ceiling. Three desks in the front row were occupied by sad Japanese businessmen who wore earphones and occasionally mouthed in tentative bewilderment.

Bernard went upstairs.

'Good morning, Mrs Franklin,' he said to the fifty-five-year-old trouser-suit behind the large manual typewriter in the outer office.

'Good morning, Mr Hopkins. Not so cold this morning.'

'No. We're lucky. Bit of an Indian summer.'

'Yes.' She composed her face into an expression of concern. 'And how's Shirley today?'

Stella Franklin always made a point of finding out the details of people's families and asking after them. She thought of this as solicitude; others had described it as nosiness.

'Much the same,' Bernard replied.

'Change in the weather doesn't make any difference to her?'

'Not really, no. I don't know what does make any difference, I'm afraid. Some days she's a lot better—it seems to be arrested—they do get these remissions, you know. Then, other days. . . .' He let the sentence trail away in a shrug.

'Still, she keeps cheerful,' said Mrs Franklin in a way that was more of a statement than a question.

'Does her best. Not much alternative.' Bernard seemed happy to leave the subject there. 'Is Mr Garrett in?'

'Oh yes.'

'May I. . . ?'

'Just go through. Liberty Hall here, Mr Hopkins. No one stands on ceremony. All open doors. No one bothers to knock.'

In spite of this licence, Bernard did tap at the door and waited for an answering 'Yeah' before going into Julian Garrett's office.

Mrs Franklin watched him go. Nice man, she thought. Very shy and correct, but his eyes were kind. Nice brown eyes. Sort of defensive, though, as if he were afraid of being hurt. Probably had been hurt, thought Mrs Franklin, who (particularly since she had been widowed) prided herself on her knowledge of human psychology and enjoyed supplying imaginative backgrounds for everyone she met. Bernard was probably a passionate man, she hazarded—yes, a passionate man who was afraid of the strength of his own feelings. Couldn't be easy for him, anyway, having a wife so ill. Mrs Franklin had read about multiple sclerosis. Must make a married life very difficult. Particularly for someone of his age. Must be around forty-five . . . still very much a man, anyway. And, however much he loved his wife, it couldn't be easy. Men have needs, Mrs Franklin knew (not so much from the evidence supplied by the late Mr Franklin as from magazines she had read which were very insistent on the subject). No, probably best thing would be if Mrs Hopkins were to suffer a sudden deterioration, go downhill very quickly and die. Then Mr Hopkins would have plenty of time to get over his bereavement and find someone else. It would give him another chance. Yes, that would be the most satisfactory thing to happen.

Having sorted out Mr Hopkins' life to her own satisfaction, Mrs Franklin continued folding the mail-shots that were to be sent out to the selection of schools in Germany which had in previous years proved such ready sources of students for the Garrettway School of Languages.

'There's really just this Turk,' said Julian Garrett languidly. His swivel-chair was tipped back, and his highly-polished black brogues rested on the edge of his paper-strewn desk. The chair and the desk were both some fifty years old, props perhaps from a thirties movie set in a newspaper office. Like the brass plate downstairs, they gave an impression of solidity, of a history stretching back longer than the school's actual five years.

The appearance of the school's principal reinforced this image of solidity. A television casting director, into whose office Julian Garrett walked, would immediately have put his name up for parts of upper-class professional men of great charm and reliability, the sort who had been to the right schools and university, and whose honour and integrity need never be questioned. The image, maintained by Julian's Savile Row suit with its discreet chalk-stripe, always put at ease those—particularly foreigners—who consulted him about their own or their children's enrolment in his school.

The fact that his appearance invited theatrical comparisons was no coincidence. Julian Garrett, who had been to the right schools and university (more or less), and whose honour and integrity had never been questioned (at least not in a court of law), had started his career as an actor and been cast in just those roles which his looks demanded. So long as the work was there, acting had suited him, not least because of the ready supply of young actresses on whom his charms could be exercised. But, after a few years in the business, the parts had, for no readily identifiable reason, got fewer. This lull in his career, happily coinciding with his mother's death and bequest to him of a considerable estate, including the house in Brighton, had pushed him towards a profession which promised to provide a more stable income than the stage. His appetite for young actresses was smoothly replaced by an appetite for young foreign students, whose two-week courses in Brighton paralleled very comfortably the short encounters of touring and provincial rep.

The school itself had been a success. After initial hiccups, it had quickly found its regular sources of students. Since very few of these had come to England and Brighton primarily for the attractions of the language course, and most of them had an exceptionally lively social life during their stays, they tended (frequently to alleviate guilt) to report back favourably to their parents on the academic standards of the Garrettway School, and so Julian did not suffer that annoyance of being judged by results which bedevils so many educational institutions.

The same lack of follow-up favoured the other side of the business, the 'cramming' of English students for resitting A-levels. Failure in the retaken examinations only confirmed for most parents what the first disappointment had gloomily prefigured, and few of them felt confident enough to make any complaint against the school.

Besides, there were successes, which could be quoted proudly in initial interviews.

Some students had given themselves such a shock by their failure that they approached resitting their exams with a new application. Some benefited from working in smaller groups or one-to-one tutorials. And, amongst the shifting ragbag of staff whom Julian Garrett employed, there were occasionally teachers with genuine gifts, who could communicate knowledge and enthusiasm to their charges.

As well as the A-level work, the Garrett-way offered to prepare students for Oxbridge entrance examinations, and this side of the business had netted for the school the perfectly respectable tally of one Exhibition and a place at Oxford, and two places at Cambridge. These achievements had been spread over the five years of Garrettway's life, but Julian, not wishing to confuse potential customers with chronology, tended (without actually lying) to imply to parents that they represented only one year's crop.

He now felt confident of the business, and lulls, like the current one, no longer caused him anxiety. Bookings for the summer courses were already up on previous years and so it was a matter of little consequence to him that he only had one Turk to offer his newest recruit to the teaching staff.

'A Turk?' Bernard Hopkins echoed.

'Yes. Been sent over here on some business course. Trouble is, as he hasn't got much language, it's all being rather lost on him at the moment.'

'So he needs an intensive course in English?'

Julian Garrett gave a wince. 'Needn't be *intensive*. Only asked for "conversational English". Just a matter of going to talk to the poor sod. Don't make a big deal of it—his company's paying.'

Detecting a slight recoil from his employee at this, Julian intensified the charm as he continued. 'I'm sorry, Bernard, if I sound cynical, but I am running a business here, not a charity. Of course, we care a lot about all our students, we want to do the best for them, but we do have to be careful.' He gave a sad, once-bitten-twice-shy shake of the head. 'I'm afraid I've had unpleasant experiences in the past. What you must do in this case is what is asked for. Give him conversational English. . . . Then, if it turns out that his grasp of the language is not even up to that, you will have to recommend an intensive course, and the necessary arrangements will be made. I'm sure the company can afford it.' There was a moment's pause. 'From what I hear of the man, I think it's quite likely that he *will* need a further course.'

'Right.' Bernard nodded, very much the dutiful employee in his new job. 'Has a time been arranged for him to come here?'

'Ah, that's one of the points. He won't be coming here. This business course he's on is pretty intensive, so I've made arrangements that our tutor will go to his hotel. He's at the Metropole. Name's Nassiri. Nine o'clock each evening, for the next fortnight. That be OK with you?'

Bernard nodded. Julian did not see that there was anything to be gained by telling him how much extra the Turk's company would be paying for this inconvenient personal service.

'Does happen from time to time,' he continued smoothly. 'Odd hours. Have to fit in with the students, though. After all, as educators, we must make them our primary concern.'

'Of course,' Bernard agreed.

'Hope that doesn't raise problems. The evenings?'

Bernard looked blank.

'With your wife. I gather she's not well.'

'Oh. No. That won't be a problem. She understands, you know, the pressures of work.'

'Good.' The principal favoured his tutor with an earnest smile. 'I do hope you're enjoying it here, finding the job OK, that sort of thing.'

'I'm enjoying it a lot. Only thing is, I don't feel really stretched at the moment. There doesn't seem to be that much work to do.'

'Time of year. Seasonal business, this. Come the summer, you just won't know how to fit all the sessions in.'

'Oh, good.' Bernard gave a little smile, as he worked round to his subject. 'Rest of the staff fairly slack too, are they?'

Julian spread out his hands. 'Not a lot around for anyone at the moment. Graham's got some Nips on the go downstairs. . . . Madeleine's got her usual A-level English casualties, one potential Oxford candidate. . . . That's about it. It'll pick up.'

'Oh yes. I wasn't worried.' Then, trying to sound casual, he asked, 'Is Madeleine in today?'

Julian didn't seem to notice anything unusual about the question. 'Think so.' He glanced at a schedule on his desk. 'Yes, she's got one of her pimply youths at eleven. She's good, you know, Madeleine. Gets results.'

Bernard nodded, smiling, and moved towards the door. Then, with strange formality, he said, 'Let's hope I can do the same.'

'Yes. Let's hope so.'

Julian flashed a grin at his departing tutor. When Bernard had gone, the grin spread. Seemed ideal, the new man. A bit naïve, obviously, but in the past Julian had found that that was a good thing. The ones who had to go were those who were too assertive, who tried to tell him how to run the place. But someone like Bernard Hopkins, undemanding, biddable, he was the sort who could be a good long-term prospect. Like Madeleine.

Julian reached for the phone. There was a young housewife in Hove who, with her children suddenly off her hands, had decided she wanted to improve herself and take a couple of A-levels. She had said she was stuck at home most of the day. He wondered if she might be free for a tutorial early that afternoon, before the children came back from school. He needed to sort something out. It was not only the business side of his life that would remain quiet until the summer influx of foreign students.

He got through and immediately recognised her voice. Deepening his own, he murmured, 'Darling. Hello. I find I'm thinking about you more than a married man should.'

Julian Garrett was not married. But he had found in the past that, when he was bringing a little romance into the lives of married women, claiming a wife of his own could prove a useful alibi, explain broken assignations and protect his privacy.

Madeleine Severn had met her pupil as she walked along the road towards the school. She recognised his tall, gangling outline ahead of her, and quickened her pace to catch up. 'Paul!' she called out.

Paul Grigson was so deep in a dream compounded of his guilt, of his sense of failure and of Madeleine Severn, that he did not at first respond when one third of it called out to him, and she had to tap him on the shoulder before she could engage his attention. 'Paul,' she repeated, more intimately.

He turned to face her, now so close to him, and his mouth dropped open at the sudden manifestation. He had, she noticed, a little crop of white spots on his inexpertly shaven chin. His nose seemed bigger than ever, and his black hair, which his mother insisted should be cut in conventional style, had been brushed up in an ineffectual attempt to achieve something more modern. He wore, as if he hated to be seen in it, a black school mackintosh, beneath which black jeans, which were tight (but not tight enough to satisfy current fashion) tapered down to white towelling socks and black slip-on shoes.

'Now, you can't pretend we're not going the same way,' said Madeleine. 'So, if you don't mind being seen in the street with your teacher. . . .'

Paul, for whom the idea was an approximation to one of his dearest fantasies, gulped that no, he didn't mind.

'Really autumnal today,' said Madeleine, and drew in the air through her nostrils.

Paul, too, took a gulp of air, but all he could smell was the sweet, flowerlike perfume of Madeleine. Adolescent despair swooped down on him, despair at the sheer impossibility of life, at the huge unbridgeable gap between his desires and their ever being fulfilled.

'Did you get that essay on 'The Eve of St Agnes' done?' asked Madeleine

'Oh yes,' said Paul. 'Yes. Yes, I did. I shouldn't think it's any good, though.'

Bernard was just coming down the stairs into the hall as the front door opened and Madeleine walked in, followed by her attendant. Bernard and Madeleine stopped. Spontaneous smiles came to both their faces. They moved towards each other and met in the middle of the black and white tiles.

'Funny, I was just thinking about you.' Bernard's words were no more than a statement. He did not infuse them with romantic emphasis as Julian Garrett might have done.

'That's nice,' said Madeleine. 'Think of the devil. . . .'

'Hardly.' He grinned awkwardly, suddenly ill-at-ease. It was as if he had been rushing headlong beyond his usual speed and had now stopped, swaying, almost over-balanced.

But Madeleine still smiled, and her smile injected another surge of that confidence which the timing of her arrival had given him. Emboldened far beyond his normal range, he found himself saying, 'Look, I have to stay in town late tonight. Got to go to the Metropole at nine, give a Turk some conversational English. I wonder if there's any chance of a drink early evening. . . ?'

The words were out, all in a rush, too quickly. He flinched in anticipation of the rebuff.

To his amazement, he saw a broader smile on Madeleine's face and heard her voice saying, 'Yes. That would be very nice.'

'What time do you finish today? Have you got an afternoon class?'

'Yes. I'm through at six.'

'Shall I meet you here?'

Madeleine shook her head gravely. The loose roll of red-gold hair quivered. 'By the entrance to West Pier. Half-past six.'

With that, not looking at him, secure in her mystery, she moved forward to one of the dark grey doors, reaching for a bunch of keys in her handbag.

Bernard was so uplifted that he was unaware of leaving the building.

Unaware, too, of the fierce hatred with which Paul Grigson's eyes burned into him as he passed.

4

'Beyond a mortal man impassion'd far
At these voluptuous accents, he arose,
Ethereal, flush'd, and like a throbbing star
Seen mid the sapphire heaven's deep repose;
Into her dream he melted, as the rose
Blendeth her odour with the violet,—
Solution   sweet: meantime   the   frost-wind
*   blows*
Like Love's alarum pattering the sharp sleet
Against the window-panes; St Agnes' moon
*   hath set.'*

Madeleine lowered the book. In her teens she had taken elocution lessons. She knew she had a good reading voice, and she had just used it. 'There now, wouldn't you agree that that's sexy?'

Paul blushed. 'I suppose it *could* be,' he offered cautiously.

'No "could" about it—it is. Keats was

the supreme poet of the senses.'

'You mean . . . sensual?' It was a word he had read in many books that had been passed around at school.

'If you like. He *felt*, he was open to sensation, and he could express it. He once wrote "let us open our leaves like a flower and be passive and receptive—budding patiently under the eye of Apollo".'

'Passive' was another word that Paul had come across in the same books, but he did not raise it as a point for discussion.

'So, you see, in 'The Eve of St Agnes', we feel the sheer power of Keats' sensuality. In that stanza he is expressing the "solution", the mingling if you like, of these two people, the ultimate togetherness in which the two of them become one. Do you understand?'

Paul thought he did. Thought even that he could contribute now to the discussion. Gulping and assuming what he hoped was a man-of-the-world air, he said, 'You mean in that stanza they, like, have it off?'

Madeleine gave a slightly petulant toss of the head, fluttering her red-gold hair. 'Whether they actually make love or not is not important. One doesn't have to be too

47

literal about poetry—particularly Keats. What I'm trying to show is how the sequence of images builds up the sensuality to a climax . . .'

Paul nodded. Another word he'd come across.

'. . . expressing the ultimate fusion, the communion of the two lovers.'

'Mmm.' Paul tried to look grave and mature and receptive, but he was finding it difficult. He always found being alone with Madeleine difficult. He was achingly numb in her presence. Her eyes seemed to see more deeply into him than any other eyes could. He was aware of her every movement, almost as if she moved at the twitching of his own nerves. He loved to be with her, spent much of the time when he was not with her thinking about being with her, and yet in her presence he hurt.

He recognised that what he was feeling was love, or a form of love, but he had never before realised the ache, the attendant hopelessness that love could bring. She was so far above him that even to think of her in that way seemed an impertinence.

There was also the physical embarrassment of being with her. Puberty, or at least

48

an awareness of it, had hit Paul Grigson late and, even as he approached his nineteenth birthday, he still felt his adult body to be an imposition, unfamiliar and dangerously booby-trapped. Thoughts of sex, ranging at lightning speed from hopelessly chaste worship of Madeleine to the crude animal displays of pornography, filled his waking mind, excluding, it seemed in moments of abject guilt, absolutely everything else. And these thoughts could move with the same lightning speed to the hair-trigger of his penis, furnishing what at times seemed a permanent erection, for which the moment was never appropriate. Indeed, for an eighteen-year-old hypersensitive virgin, there are few appropriate moments. The relief of masturbation, seized greedily in bed night or morning, or, more alarmingly, in lavatories (or anywhere else he believed to be private) at any time of the day, brought only brief respite and stirred such a foul brew of guilt and self-abasement that it could not be considered a satisfactory solution.

When he was with Madeleine, the erection seemed perpetual. In spite of the nobility and chastity of his feelings towards her, it stood fixed in mockery of him, causing constant embarrassment. He was aware of the maturity of the tutorial situation, teacher and pupil facing each other in chairs, but he longed desperately to regress to the safety of school, where a desk would shield his decency. He made much of positioning books and notes on his lap, but they did little to alleviate the discomfort.

Madeleine was blithely unaware of her charge's problem, but Paul didn't know that and assumed that every look she cast in his direction pierced through to the root of his shame. This compounded and added a physical dimension to the pain he felt in her presence.

Madeleine looked at her watch. 'Oh dear. Gone over again. Look, I don't want to leave Keats yet. I'd like you to have a look at. . . .'

She gave him his next task, and Paul scribbled distracted notes on the pad held firmly against his lap. Then Madeleine rose and crossed to the door.

Gingerly Paul got to his feet. With some discomfort, and an adjusting hand in his pocket, he followed his idol out of the room.

As he walked disconsolately home, Paul

suddenly realised that Keats *was* sexy.

Sexy, yes, but *pure* sexy. That was it. Madeleine had been right. The lovers hadn't had it off in that stanza she quoted. Their . . . what was the word she'd used? . . . communion, yes . . . their communion had been too total, too spiritual to sink to mere orgasm. Their love didn't need any shabby carnal encounter. It was above all that.

It was like his love for Madeleine, something pure and sanctified. He felt a surge of confidence. He saw the way ahead for their relationship. It would be inspired by pure devotion, not sullied with lust. And that would make it stronger. They would reach heights of love unknown to those who merely indulged their bodies.

He felt purged by the thought. A new dedication, a new meaning, a (had he known the word) new asceticism had come into his life. His erection, he noted with satisfaction, had respectfully withdrawn. No more masturbation, no more lust, just pure devotion from now on.

He almost bounced up the garden path, as he took his front-door key out of his pocket.

As soon as he was inside, the noise from the sitting-room reminded him that Bob was there. Bob had been a friend from the comprehensive, who had gone off to work in a warehouse when Paul had moved on (with limited success, as it proved) to Sixth Form College to take his A-levels. They had stayed in touch, maintaining a loose friendship based more on habit than on any surviving common interest. Bob had appeared at about ten that morning, after Paul's mother had gone off to work, saying that he had the day off and he'd got a video he wanted to watch, and Paul wouldn't mind, would he, if Bob used the VCR. Paul said he wouldn't mind, but he thought his mother might. Bob said no problem, he'd be away long before she got back, go on, it'd be all right, and Paul had said, not without misgiving but without a valid reason for refusal, well, OK.

Being with Madeleine had put all of this from his mind.

As he pushed open the sitting-room door, he saw that it wasn't just Bob who was watching the video. Three pairs of eyes turned guiltily towards him. The other two belonged to Tony Ashton and Sam Clegg, who had both also been at the comprehensive, friends of Bob's rather than Paul's, and who were now on the dole with, presumably, plenty of mornings to idle away watching videos. All three faces relaxed when they saw that the arrival was Paul and not his mother.

But it wasn't the party of spectators that caught Paul's attention as he walked in. On the television screen which faced the door was a close-up of a woman's mouth doing things to a man which he had only read about in books. A blurred sound-track of sighs and slaverings accompanied her movements.

'Like what you see, Grigson?' Tony's voice demanded coarsely. 'Blimey, look at him—goggling like a bleeding frog.'

With a sick feeling of shame, Paul realised that his erection, so recently banished for ever, had sprung back to attention. He dragged his eyes away from the screen to the three sprawled with their backs against his mother's sofa. There were beer-cans and empty crisp packets on the floor. 'Look, you shouldn't be here. I said Bob could come and watch a video, I didn't say you two could.'

'What difference does it make?' asked Tony.

'Well . . .' The words were out before he could stop them. 'My mother wouldn't like it.'

'Oh dear, oh lor',' said Tony in a mocking voice. 'What a blooming disaster. Mummy wouldn't like it. Mustn't do anything Mummy wouldn't like, must we? You great wally. I bet your bloody Mum still bleeding tucks you in at night.'

Paul just managed to stop himself from denying this charge. 'It's not just her. I don't want you making a mess of this place either. I didn't invite you.'

'Oh, shut it. What harm are we doing?' Tony reached with his left hand for a beer-can.

'Well, I don't like the idea of you swilling beer and indulging your fantasies all over my sitting-room.'

'Indulging my fantasies, eh?' Tony echoed, imitating Paul's slightly prissy tone. 'Listen, Grigson, I don't need fantasies, because I'm seeing Tracey Ruskin tonight. I'm just watching this to get some ideas of what she can do for me, that's all.'

This reference brought Paul's eyes back

54

to the screen. Another naked man had appeared from somewhere and the woman's mouth was now sharing its attentions between the two of them.

'If Tracey's going to do *that* for you,' said Sam, who was a bit of a humorist, 'can I be the other feller?'

This was greeted by appropriately raucous laughter. The close-up on the screen opened out to reveal the three bodies and show what the two men were doing to the woman. Paul edged forward, mesmerised, to sit on the arm of the sofa.

He had never seen anything like it before. The books had shown stills of everything that was being done, but to see it in motion, to hear the sighs and grunts. . . . The pressure on his trousers was intolerable, threatening disgrace. He felt a kind of uncleanness, a nausea, but he could not shift his eyes from the screen.

'Good bit coming,' commented Tony, who had clearly seen the video a few times before.

'Coming? Who?' asked Sam, who had his comic reputation to maintain.

This was unpleasantly apposite for Paul, who was having great difficulty in keeping his hand away from his crutch.

'Never guess who's about to push his way in through the door,' continued Tony, the expert. 'Only the bleeding Alsatian.' His guffaw was echoed by the others.

The Alsatian arrived, and more plotless permutations ensued. Paul's shock and arousal became tempered by boredom, but he knew that all these scenes would be locked in his memory and be summoned up to enrich his future fantasies. Keats and Madeleine were figures from another world.

Abruptly, with no conclusion either artistic or logical, the tape ended. 'Not bad, eh?' said Tony with proprietorial satisfaction.

'Woman was a bit of a boot,' observed Sam.

'Yeah, but who cares what she looks like when she does all that,' said Bob.

'Probably a whore,' announced Tony with authority. 'Looks like she done it a few times before, doesn't she?'

'You ever been to a whore, Tony?'

' 'Course I have. Only lost my bleeding virginity to one, didn't I? When I was fourteen,' he lied, and then added, with bravado, 'She taught me a few things I haven't forgotten.'

'That's the sort of woman you want, eh? Like that one in the video.' Bob leered. 'Doesn't say a bleeding word and just keeps doing it to you.'

'Tracey Ruskin's pretty much like that,' said Tony.

'Yeah. Not much of a one for the conversation. I remember from school.'

'Got better things to do with her mouth, eh?' Sam came in bang on cue and was rewarded by his tribute of laughter.

Tony turned to look at Paul, an insolent smile at the corner of his mouth. 'How's your sex-life, eh, Grigson?'

'Mustn't grumble,' he said, with an attempt at insouciant bravado.

'No? Good. Still seeing that Sharon Wilkinson?'

'From time to time.'

'Always looked a tight-arsed little virgin to me.'

'Appearances can be deceptive.' Paul added what he hoped was a light laugh.

'Oh yeah. She put out for you then, does she?'

'You'd be surprised.'

But the note of mystery didn't satisfy Tony Ashton. 'Yes, I bleeding would. That's why I'm asking. Go on, does she do it for you?'

Paul rose from the sofa. 'Look, we'd better clean this place up.'

Tony's hand shot up, grabbed him by the arm and pulled him back down. Their faces came close; Paul was very aware of the perforation in Tony's ear-lobe from which a silver cross dangled. 'I'm asking, Grigson.'

'Well, I'm not telling you, Ashton. You bloody well mind your own business!'

Tony released his grasp and slumped back with a sardonic grin. 'I see. Think I got the message. Dead romantic, I bet you are, Grigson. When you and Sharon Wilkinson go out together, it's not just one virgin, it's a bleeding convention of them.'

'That's not true!' Paul protested, swamped by blushes.

'No. No, of course it isn't.' But Tony Ashton's expression belied his words. He looked insolently into Paul's eyes until his victim turned away. Then he seemed to lose interest in the baiting. 'Here, Bob, did you bring that other video, one you talked about?'

'Sure.' Bob reached into a plastic carrier bag and pulled out an unmarked cassette-box. 'Bloke in the shop said it was pretty strong stuff. Been banned in a good few countries.'

'Oh yeah. Let's have a butcher's then. Wind back the porno, Clegg.'

'Look,' Paul began to protest feebly, 'I really don't think you should start watching another one. I think you ought to be going. I—'

'Shut it, Grigson,' Tony Ashton hissed.

The old cassette was taken out and the new one loaded. The screen crackled with snow for a few moments, then, without any of the copyright claims and injunctions that would have shown it to be a legal tape, a picture suddenly appeared and simultaneously a woman's scream burst from the television's speaker.

The scene appeared to be a school, but it was night-time and one could not be sure. The girl who had screamed was wearing a kind of school uniform, but the blouse was ripped, showing the shadow of young breasts. Tears ran down her cheeks and a gout of blood welled from her broken lip as she backed hysterically away from the camera. Through her screams two other sounds could be heard, the regular pant of masculine breathing and the juddering whine of a two-stroke petrol-engine.

As the girl backed away against a wall, a blurred line rose from the bottom of the screen. It was only when the shot widened to reveal the orange machine held in black gloved hands that this line could be identified as a whirring blade of a circular saw. It drew closer to the girl, and closer.

Then it made a sudden lunge towards the cowering figure. The girl screamed and threw herself sideways. With a shriek of metal on plaster, the blade jarred against the wall. The camera showed the long scar in the paintwork, and, alongside, a spray of glistening blood-drops.

It swung away from the wall to the corner where the girl now slumped, clutching at her shoulder with fingers through which blood spurted. The snarling line of the saw-blade moved inexorably towards her. Now she had no resistance to offer but screams, and these grew in pitch and mixed to gurgles as the blade scythed again and again across her young flesh.

The watchers knew it was trickery. They knew there had been editing and cross-cutting between fantasy and reality, between the human actress and the flesh and entrails of some animal, but the splattering blood and splintering bone still held them transfixed in silence.

Paul gaped like the others. The sense of pollution was again with him, but nothing could have induced him to shift his eyes from the screen.

And, though he was too preoccupied to worry about it at that moment, he was subsequently to undergo a great deal of anxiety about the fact that his erection had returned, stronger than ever.

5

It was half-past two before Paul could get rid of his uninvited guests and their unsettling cargo of videos. He tidied the sitting-room the moment they had gone, sweeping up the crisp crumbs with a brush and dust-pan, and burying the empty beer-cans under the rest of the contents of the dustbin. He worked with fierce concentration, trying to home his mind back on to the vision of purity with Madeleine which had been so clear when he arrived at the house, but he knew he was failing and knew that it was only a matter of time before he went into the lavatory or his bedroom to summon up his new stock of fantasies and achieve brief, inadequate relief.

He was just about to go upstairs when he saw the outline of a figure through the frosted glass of the front door. He heard the key in the lock and his mother entered.

He felt a shock of guilt. God, if she had come in twenty minutes earlier. . . . But why had she come, anyway? She worked full-time as a secretary at the university and was not usually home till six at the earliest. She looked tired and pale.

'You all right, Mum?'

'Not too hot. That's why I came home early.'

With frightening speed, his mind filled with images of her being terminally ill, of her just having had cancer diagnosed, of her only having three months to live. By the time he spoke again, he had just been to her cremation.

'Is it something serious?' he asked anxiously.

She gave a weary shake of her head. 'No, Paul. Nothing serious. Just off-colour. You know, ordinary things. . . .'

He did not probe further. He had a feeling that she was talking about the appalling mystery of menstruation; he did not wish to be drawn into explanations and consequent embarrassment. His mother was in her late forties and there were things going on with her that he did not fully understand or wish to have defined.

'I think I'll go up and have a lie-down,' said his mother. 'How did your lesson go this morning?'

'Oh, fine, I think. We did Keats.'

'You seem to keep doing Keats.'

'The Romantics are very important.'

Mrs Grigson snorted. 'Well, I just hope it's doing you some good. God knows they charge enough at that place.' She could never let him forget how much his comparative failure in his A-levels had cost her, both in disappointment and in hard cash. Paul often wished she would just give up the idea of his ever getting to university. Very few of his friends from the comprehensive had even gone on to Sixth Form College, and the people there who'd failed their exams had accepted the world's assessment of them with dignity, not pressed on in the face of the evidence, trying to change their fates. God knows, he thought, if I'm not good enough to qualify on A-levels, what chance have I got in the Oxford exams? The colleges there are supposed to be looking for exceptional minds; when they find those, then maybe they're prepared to forget about A-levels. But mine's not an exceptional mind. I know it isn't.

He wished his father was still alive. Then it would have been all right. The old man had never had a lot of time for education. But his death had released in Mrs Grigson a latent intellectual snobbery, which had been exacerbated when she started working at the university. Most of the lecturers she worked for there assumed that everyone went on to further education, and she quickly became determined that, like it or not, her son was going to have the benefits (on the precise nature of which she was a little vague) of university. And when Mrs Grigson was determined about something, Paul, like his father before him, offered about as much resistance as a daisy in the path of a tank.

'No, I think I am learning a lot,' he protested. 'Sort of seeing different ways of seeing things, getting a different approach. . . .'

Another snort from his mother. 'So long as it's an approach that gets you through the exams. You've still got the same tutor for English?'

'Yes.'

'With the strange name.'

'Miss Severn.'

'That's right. Where on earth do you get

a name like that?'

Paul replied with awe, 'She says she thinks the family's descended from Joseph Severn, who was with Keats when he died.'

'Oh yes?' Mrs Grigson was unimpressed by this possible link with literary history. 'I hope to God she's teaching you something. Only time I met her, she seemed too airy-fairy for words.'

Before Paul could even contemplate leaping to the defence of his idol, his mother went on. 'Still, at least it's the same tutor. Let's hope the continuity helps. I have my reservations about that Garrettway place. Think I should have shopped around a bit first. No one at the university seems to have heard of it.'

'I'm sure it's fine.'

'Should be at those prices.' Once again the guilt-trigger of money. In fact, ever since he could remember, everything his mother had said or done had triggered guilt in Paul. Her version of swamping, martyred love had made him feel guilty for existing, certainly guilty for being male, in some obscure way even guilty for the fact that his father had died, guilty for the suffering that reorganising her life on her own had caused his mother. At that moment he felt guilty for her feeling off-colour, as if he were responsible for the incomprehensible operations of her body.

Mrs Grigson stopped halfway up the stairs. 'You haven't forgotten you've got a driving lesson at five?'

He had, but he denied it. The events of the day had put the lesson from his mind, and he felt a little inward sag at the recollection. He knew that being able to drive was necessary, and that in time he would feel the benefit, but he hated the lessons, hated the sarcastic wit of his instructor, hated his own ineptitude, hated being taught yet again, hated being pushed.

'And what do you want for supper tonight?' She stretched her neck round to ease some muscular pain. 'I dare say I'll be well enough to cook something.'

'I don't want anything. I'll just grab a sandwich when I get back from the lesson.'

'Oh?' Mrs Grigson could put volumes of interrogation into that single syllable.

'I'm going out.'

'Ah.'

'Meeting someone. I'm sure I told you.'

'I don't remember your doing so.'

'I'm sure I did.'

'Well, I don't remember your telling me who it is you are meeting.' His mother's eyes transfixed him.

'Sharon,' he mumbled.

'Sharon. Oh, Sharon Wilkinson. The publican's daughter. Star of the Boots check-out counter.' Since she had been working at the university, Mrs Grigson had no time for people who had left school without any O-levels. 'That should be a stimulating evening, shouldn't it, Paul?'

He didn't reply.

His mother let out a brisk sigh. 'Well, maybe I won't see you in your brief sandwich-break at six. I may not bother to get up just for that pleasure. But do remember I worry if you're not back by half-past eleven.' She moved up a couple more stairs. 'And do be sensible with dear little Sharon, won't you?'

'What do you mean?'

'It's not my place to pry into what you get up to with your girl-friends, Paul, but it's obvious you can't be going out with this one for her conversation. All I'm saying is— I just don't think I could cope with your having to get married to someone with the intellectual abilities of Sharon Wilkinson.'

With her fingers to her temple as a reminder that she was not feeling at all well, Mrs Grigson went upstairs to bed. Leaving her son with more threads of guilt and misery to knit into the tangled circuitry of his mind.

As he walked towards Sharon's house, Paul felt sick with tension. It would all be a disaster, he knew. He would throw up over her as soon as she opened the door.

God, why did he get so uptight about everything? Sharon was nothing, nothing to get in this state over. Just a girl, moderately pretty, no more, and moderately thick. If there was any reason for seeing her, it was just because she was a girl, because boys were meant to go out with girls. Or for sex. He swallowed, tasting the sourness of vomit.

If only he could keep her in proportion. If only he could keep anything in proportion. When he was with her, he knew she was just a rather ordinary girl, but when he was on his own, she, like everything else in his life, took on grotesque forms, became extreme, too important, not important enough, too keen on him, not keen enough on him, too attractive, too ugly. He could never bridge the gulf between her reality and his fantasies of her.

Sex was the answer. It must be. He should just have her, callously have her, and that would get her in proportion. Then he'd be able to be objective about her. He needed sex. He had a right to it. Everyone else seemed to just grab it without agonising. Why shouldn't he?

And women did want it. All the books said they did. Incongruous though it might seem, through all the demureness and all those strange guilt-inspiring things their bodies did, they must want it. Perhaps Sharon even panted for his image in her bed at night as he did for hers (or at least for an image which was hard to fix specifically, but to which she certainly contributed).

Scenes from the day's first video sprang into his mind, registering instantly on the antenna between his legs. That woman had wanted it. She'd been bloody desperate for it. All women were probably just like that underneath. Sharon, too.

It was nearly half-past six. Her parents would be out down at the pub. She'd be on her own when he arrived. Panting for it.

Yes, that's what he should do—go in, close the door behind him, push her into the sitting-room, back on to the sofa, and have her. Never mind if she protested, he should do it, it was his right. Anyway, Tony Ashton had told him that girls always meant yes when they said no. They just got a charge out of teasing. Yes, he would have her, and then she'd have some respect for him.

He walked up her garden path and rang the doorbell. Then he dropped his hands to shield the front of his trousers.

The door opened, and Sharon stood there, wearing a coat and holding a handbag. She looked very ordinary. On her chin the flake of a spot was inadequately covered with make-up.

'Hello, Paul. Knew you'd be on time, so I got my coat on.'

'Oh.'

'Shall we go then?'

'Yes. Fine.'

They walked in single file back down the garden path.

6

Paul and Sharon took a bus down into the town. They had been out together some half-dozen times and, though the relationship did not seem to have progressed much since the first date, a sort of pattern had emerged. Both would have eaten at home; they did not have enough money to think of going out for meals. Paul was, after all, still a student and dependent on pocket money and subs from his mother. Sharon was earning, but was by nature parsimonious and, when she had paid her parents for her accommodation, put most of the rest of her wage-packet into a building society account. She thought ahead (although Paul did not realise it) to mortgages and fitted kitchens and matching bathroom suites. No individual was as yet involved in these projections of her future, but she assessed Paul, as she did every boy she went out with, for husband potential. She approved of the lack of flamboyance in his entertainment of her, which she put down to shrewd money management rather than poverty. She approved less of the idea of his still being a student and contemplating university. She was eighteen and reckoned she should be married before she hit twenty. And whoever she married must have a nice secure job. Three years at university could only be three years off a company promotion ladder, and the old argument that people with higher qualifications got better jobs no longer, according to her father's assessment of the economic situation, held water.

But Paul was someone to go out with. He was polite, sometimes amusing, and he didn't keep grabbing at her all the time, like most boys. Sometimes she didn't understand a word of what he was talking about, but, until such time as someone better came along, she was quite content to go out for safe, predictable evenings with him.

When they got into town, they would usually go to a pub, paying round and round about, talking intermittently and making three drinks last an evening. Once or twice they had met friends from school and got into a crowd. Sharon liked that. She liked having a few laughs with a crowd. Paul appeared not to.

Other times they might go to the cinema, sharing the price of the tickets. Sharon quite liked the cinema, so long as there wasn't anything violent or sexy in the films. She liked a good story, something a bit romantic, preferably with Shirley MacLaine crying in it. The couple of times they had been, Paul had been polite enough to consult her tastes and they had seen her sort of film.

She didn't get the impression that Paul had liked the films as much as she had, but she let him hold her hand and put his arm round her, so he couldn't really complain. She even let his hand rest, for five minutes or so, on her breast, but when it strayed to her waistband or lower, she had said no. And he hadn't tried again, which was nice, and unlike certain other boys she had been out with who spent all their time trying to get inside her clothes and to whom she had had to become quite unpleasant. She was not going to get caught that way. In her projections of her future, along with the mortgage, the fitted kitchen and the matching bathroom suite, was a virginity to be yielded on her wedding night and not before.

At the end of their evenings together, usually about half-past ten, they would catch a bus up from the front and Paul would walk her home from the bus-stop. On her doorstep they would linger, though she would not allow the lingering to last too long because of the neighbours. He would put his arms on her shoulders and, gauchely holding her at a distance so that she could not feel his shame, he would give her wet and inexpert kisses. She was quite prepared to invite him in for a cup of coffee, but since he never asked, and since she knew that cups of coffee on the sofa could lead to awkward extrications, she was happy to leave well enough alone, and didn't raise the matter.

Paul would then leave. Sharon would have a bath and, neat in her crisp little nightdress in her crisp little bed, she would read her latest Mills and Boon romance for about twenty minutes before going to sleep, to dream of mortgages, fitted kitchens, matching bathroom suites and, perhaps, the tall dark-haired man with steely blue eyes who had just sent roses to the heroine of her book.

Paul, on the other hand, would go home in a state of new turbulence, and, in the sweaty creases of his bed, graft the recent memory of Sharon's lips on to the composite fantasy woman who directed the desperate movements of his hand.

That evening they sat on the top of the bus as usual, and as usual Paul asked Sharon how work had gone, and she, as usual but with minor variations, told him how a Frenchman had come in and bought some hair lacquer that he thought was deodorant and how the store detective had stopped an old lady who tried to walk out with a jar of bath-salts.

Then she asked him how his studying was going. She did this only out of politeness. At school her only concern had been how soon she could leave and get a job, but she was well brought up and she knew you had to show an interest.

'All right, I think,' Paul replied. 'I've got this very good teacher.'

The image of Madeleine, her red-gold hair loose and flowing, flashed across his mind, and he felt a pang of disloyalty for being with Sharon.

'We've been working on Keats,' he continued.

'Oh yes?' said Sharon.

'Good stuff. Have you read any?'

She shook her head. 'Don't think so. What's he write?'

'Well, he's a Romantic, really.'

'Oh.' She grew animated. 'I might have read some of his things then. I read a lot of that. Is he in Mills and Boon?'

'No. No, he was a poet. Early nineteenth century. Died young.'

'Oh.' The animation was replaced by indifference. Paul was deeply embarrassed by her ignorance. He felt exposed, as if he were responsible for her, as if he would be judged by her.

'Reading a good one at the moment,' said Sharon. 'It's set on Crete. Sounds really nice. I'd like to go to Crete. They have wonderful sunsets there, apparently.'

'Oh.'

'You ever been there? Crete, or Greece?'

Paul shook his head.

'Girl I work with went to Corfu. Ipsos. Lovely she said it was. Really good discos they have. Every night. I like discos,' she added wistfully.

Well, it was worth trying. She had expressed her liking for discos to Paul before. She thought going to one might enliven their dates. She enjoyed dancing in public, showing off the steps she practised so assiduously in front of her bedroom mirror. But, from what he said, Paul didn't seem to like discos. So far he had not risen to any of her suggestions.

That evening's met the same lack of response. Accepting this philosophically, Sharon went on with the plot of the book she was reading. 'You see, what happens is this feller's in Crete on business and he meets this English girl, Virginia, who's out there working as a courier and he falls for her and they have this amazing evening where they just walk along the sand and talk and, you know, it really works, it's the real thing. And he fixes to meet her the next evening, but when he gets to this restaurant where they fixed to meet—"taverna" they call it in the book—that's Greek for restaurant, I think—anyway, he sees her dancing very close with this Greek. And he's furious and goes off, but he doesn't realise that this Greek is one of the owners of the company that Virginia works for and, you know, although it looks sexy, in fact they're just being friendly. And the trouble is, he—this feller, the Englishman, Randall he's called—he's going back to England the next day, and so Virginia rushes off from this taverna place to try and find him and explain, but he's checked out of his hotel and when she gets to the airport, she finds he's taken an earlier flight and he's gone.'

She pronounced this with finality. 'So what happens?' asked Paul.

'That's as far as I've got,' admitted Sharon. 'But I know it'll be all right. They'll get together in the end.'

'How do you know that?'

'They always do.'

'Doesn't it make it a bit boring, knowing what's going to happen?'

Sharon looked at him curiously. He really did say the oddest things at times. 'No, that's what's nice about it.'

'Oh.'

'Happy endings are nice. Does that feller you was talking about—Keats—do his poems have happy endings?'

'Don't think so, much. There's a lot about death in his poems, death and love going together, Pleasure and Pain, you know.'

Sharon shivered. 'Don't think I'd like it much. My Mum always says there's enough nasty things in the world without people writing about them.'

Paul couldn't think of anything to say to that. There was a silence. Then, for something to do, he reached out impulsively and took her hand. She did not seem to mind and gave his a reassuring squeeze. Greatly daring, he leant across and brushed his lips against hers. They were warm and seemed possibly to open slightly at the contact. He was instantly aroused, though, in a sitting posture, this did not cause him problems.

He looked into her clear blue eyes, blank as boiled sweets. 'You've got nice eyes,' he said.

'Thank you.' She gave his hand a friendly squeeze.

Emboldened, he continued, 'In fact, all of you's nice. You're just nice.'

'So are you,' said Sharon, to be polite.

He leant across and placed his large lips on hers, which parted slightly and pressed back with some enthusiasm. Sharon did not mind being kissed in public. In fact, in many ways she felt safer being kissed in public than when she was alone with a feller. On the top of a bus there was no danger of anything going too far, so she was prepared to be responsive.

Paul misread the reason for her warmth. He felt suddenly ecstatic, uplifted. She really fancies me, he thought. She's really panting for me. She wants me. Right, tonight's the night. We won't go to the cinema, we'll just have a few drinks, get her a bit tanked up, then back to her place, I'll ask to come in for a coffee, and then we'll *do it,* quick, before her Mum and Dad get back from the pub. The restaurant part keeps going after closing-time, they're never back till after midnight, I've got plenty of time. She wants it, too, no question about that. God, the time I've wasted. Should have got in there straight away.

He drew back from the kiss, smiled and leant forward for another little peck. She smiled back, a nice, safe, domestic smile. He looked out of the window. 'Hey, we're there!'

He grabbed her hand and they scampered down the stairs, both feeling good, full of youth. On the pavement, he put his arm round her shoulder and planted a little kiss on her cheek.

'You are nice,' he repeated, incapable of further invention.

'So are you,' she repeated, polite again.

Relief flooded through him. It was going to be all right. She fancied him.

Pulling her by the hand, he ran down towards the pub. Sharon, who thought he was behaving a bit oddly but couldn't see that there was any harm in it, ran along with him.

The euphoria lasted into the pub. Paul felt in charge, felt for the first time for ages that he was dictating events rather than being dictated to. 'Don't think we'll go to the flicks,' he said authoritatively. 'Just have a few drinks.'

'All right.' Sharon was disappointed. There was a Shirley MacLaine picture on at the ABC ONE that her friend at work had said was frightfully sad, and Sharon had really quite fancied seeing that. But on a date it should really be the feller's decision, she supposed, so she'd better go along with what he said.

'Then maybe back to your place for a coffee,' Paul continued, atypically brave.

'All right.' Sharon acquiesced to that idea too, but she was aware of the warning sign. Still, she'd been lucky with Paul so far and, if he did try anything on, she felt confident she could handle it. She'd dealt with much more persistent boys in the past. And it was only to be expected. Paul had been slower than most, but there came a time when all of them, for reasons she recognised but did not fully understand, seemed to want a bit of a cuddle on the sofa. She would just ensure that it wasn't more than a cuddle.

'So what are you drinking?'

'I'll have a bitter lemon, thank you, Paul.'

'Oh, come on. Have a gin in it.'

Another warning sign. 'A bitter lemon, thank you, Paul,' she repeated, with some asperity. 'On its own.'

He couldn't argue further. She went to find a seat in one of the booths along the walls, while he ordered the drinks. He got her bitter lemon and, rather than his usual light ale, a whisky for himself. He didn't like the taste much, but he thought he might need a bit of bolstering that evening. When it was put down on the counter, the whisky looked very small, so he asked for a double. That still looked small, so he drowned it in water. He was surprised how much it cost.

'What's that you're drinking?' Sharon asked suspiciously as he sat down.

'Whisky,' he replied with some bravado.

'I see,' she said, recognising a third warning sign. But she did not stop him from taking her hand.

'You're nice,' he said, still stuck for a development of the compliment.

This time she didn't reciprocate, but that didn't worry him. His confidence was overweeningly high. It was going to work. He would just be firm and it would happen.

There was silence between them. Silence never worried Sharon. In fact, very little worried Sharon. There were things in life which she recognised to be annoyances, but she knew how to deal with them.

Into their silence came conversation from the invisible occupants of the adjoining booth. A man's voice. 'Yes, it is sad, but one learns to accept it. One learns to accept everything, I suppose, after a time. I suppose that's what happened with my marriage. I've just accepted that there's something that used to be in my life and is no longer there. Nothing good seems to last.'

A woman's voice. ' " Joy, whose hand is ever at his lips, Bidding adieu." '

Paul was electrified. Sharon winced at the involuntary squeeze he gave to her hand. 'What's the matter?'

But he only had ears for the conversation behind him. He took a gulp of the watery whisky.

'Yes,' said the man's voice. 'Love can die. Or be killed by external circumstances.'

'Or,' said Madeleine's voice, thick with emotion, 'the one you love can die, and the love itself can stay alive.'

'And never be transferred to someone else?'

'It would take a long time. And maybe it would not be the same love.'

'No. Maybe not.' But the man's voice sounded happy rather than sad.

They sank into their own silence. 'What *is* the matter with you?' asked Sharon, breaking the other silence.

'Nothing. I just think. . . . You'd really like to see that movie, wouldn't you?'

'Well, yes, but if you'd rather—'

'Let's go.' Paul rose abruptly. 'We'll just get there if we. . . .'

His voice trailed away as he heard Madeleine's saying, 'I'll get us another drink. No, really, it is my turn.'

There was no escape. He stood transfixed as she rounded the corner of the booth. She looked to him more beautiful than ever, the wonderful hair loose, a heightened flush on the cheeks beneath those violet-blue eyes.

'Paul. Hello. What a surprise.'

He mouthed hopelessly.

'Aren't you going to introduce me to your friend?'

'We, er, were just going.'

Madeleine looked at him quizzically, demanding a response.

'Yes. Right. This is Sharon. Sharon Wilkinson. Sharon—Miss Severn, my, er . . . my teacher.'

'Pleased to meet you,' said Sharon, with a common little nod.

'Where are you two off to?' Madeleine didn't mean it to sound patronising, but it made Paul feel about eleven. He looked at Sharon and, by comparison with the older woman, she seemed gawky, unformed, vulgar.

'Flicks,' Sharon replied. 'Shirley MacLaine movie. Supposed to be dead romantic.'

'Oh. Well, have a good evening.' With a little smile, Madeleine moved across to the bar.

'Thank you,' said Paul.

'Nice to meet you,' Sharon called out politely.

Crimson with shame, Paul scuttled out of the pub. Bewildered and disowned, Sharon followed.

'I think it was all right,' said Madeleine as she handed Bernard his drink.

'What do you mean?'

'That was one of my Garrettway students. I don't think he saw you, though.'

'Well, why shouldn't he. . . ?'

'Your wife,' Madeleine murmured conspiratorially. 'We don't want anything to get back to her. If it gets round Garrettway, Mrs Franklin's such a frightful gossip. . . .'

Bernard Hopkins felt obscurely pleased. Madeleine's desire for secrecy meant that she saw the meeting as more than just two colleagues having a drink, implied perhaps that she felt a little for him of what he was feeling for her. There was complicity, contact. He felt happy.

As he walked from the pub to his Turk in

the Metropole Hotel, Bernard's thoughts were more complex. The happiness was still there, but it was overshadowed by fears. He shouldn't have talked to Madeleine so much about his wife. He should have kept that part of his life out of it.

There had been other women, other failures which he did not like to dwell on. But for none of them had he felt like this. Surely with Madeleine it would work. The feeling he had for her was so strong, he felt a sense of rightness. Madeleine would make him feel like a normal man again.

But he must go very gently, very slowly, very carefully. Make plans. This one was too good to mess up.

Paul and Sharon's evening, which had begun so promisingly, turned into disaster. He didn't speak to her on the way to the cinema, he didn't touch her during the film, and he didn't speak to her on the bus back.

Finally, when he deposited her on her doorstep, she fixed her blank blue eyes on his. 'Paul, what's the matter? What have I done?'

'Nothing,' he said. 'You haven't done

anything.' He let out a rasp of laughter and walked away.

Sharon was more puzzled than hurt. Her self-esteem was very durable. She had a bath, got into her crisp little nightdress and into her crisp little bed and read about how Randall and Virginia finally re-met, sorted out the confusions of Crete, and faced the rest of their lives together.

Paul walked home in fury. How could he ever think of another woman while Madeleine was alive? He felt destroyed, guilty about the lust he had felt for Sharon, desolate for being away from Madeleine, anguished at his hopeless youth and inexperience.

And furious at the man who had been with her. He had not looked into the booth, but he had heard the assignation being made that morning. His rival was the new tutor at Garrettway.

Two things he wanted to do with desperate urgency.

The first was to rid himself of the terrible handicap of his virginity.

The second was to kill the man who was after Madeleine Severn.

As he passed a tree, he swung his arm at it and smashed his right hand in a karate chop against the rough bark.

The shock went through his entire body. He held up the crippled hand in the street light. The skin was broken and, even as he looked at it, he could see the fleshy pad of his palm begin to swell.

And the pain he felt gave him pleasure.

7

He knew now what had to be done and, having made the decision, he felt calmer. It was ridiculous that he had left it so long. All his contemporaries, he knew from what they had said, had disposed of this insignificant rite years before. And yet for him it had always seemed so difficult, such a big deal. Well, maybe if love were involved, it would be a big deal. That was the main argument for making it a simple, clinical, financial transaction, paying for his passport into the real adult world.

So it had to be a prostitute. On some nameless tart he would finally unload the insupportable encumbrance of his virginity. Just as a dry run, just to prove that he could do it, that technically everything worked. It would be easier with no emotion involved. And then, after the anonymous initiation, he would be ready for the real thing, ready for Madeleine.

To his mind, a prostitute meant London. He had seen the scribbled names on bell pushes when he walked round Soho, the felt-penned phone numbers scrawled on coinboxes at Victoria Station. No doubt similar services were available in Brighton, but he didn't know where to start looking for them. Besides, it had to be secret. There were people in Brighton who might recognise him. And a trip to London, bracketed by the train journeys, would put the episode outside his normal life, an important, a necessary act, but one of which he could forget the details, one that he could quickly push to the back of his mind.

It was a course he had contemplated before, but never with this determination.

The house was empty as he made his preparations. Obviously he needed some disguise. Not only would it prevent recognition, it would also give him a role, distance him from the act, as if what was being done was being done by someone else.

In the loft there were two suitcases full of his father's clothes. After his father died, his mother had emptied the wardrobe into these cases, intending at some later date to sort them through to sell or give to charity. But the second part of the plan had never been achieved. As she slowly recovered from the shock of bereavement, she had felt less and less willing to stir up painful thoughts, and so the clothes had stayed hidden away, unsorted.

Her son had looked through them before, when contemplating other acts of secrecy, so he was able to go straight to what he wanted. He had even tried some of the garments on and found, to his surprise, that now his frame had filled out a little, they fitted remarkably well. Or maybe it was just that his father was larger in his memory than he had been in reality.

In his mind he had preselected the brown herring-bone sports jacket and dark grey flannel trousers which he had worn before. Their cut was a bit dated, but not so much as to be conspicuous. Plenty of people still walked around in clothes like that, people to whom no one in the street would give a second glance, and that was exactly the kind of anonymity he sought. He took the garments out of the suitcase and looked at them. They remained ideal for his purpose. Around them still clung a hint of the nicotine smell of his dead father, something that he found both unnerving and strangely comforting.

But the weather was colder than on the previous occasions when he had dressed up in the costume. He would need an overcoat. That he had not investigated. He couldn't wear his own; the effect of secrecy would be ruined. He opened the second suitcase.

There was a duffel-coat in there, familiar, camel-coloured with rough string loops and wooden toggles. It was perfect, again inconspicuous, anonymous. And the hood could be useful, providing additional cover.

But there were other objects in the case that were more moving. Into it his mother had thrown not just clothes, but also his father's private possessions, the details, the props by which the son had identified the man. There was the shaving-kit, badger-hair brush and the slim-necked silver safety razor, at the top of which, with a twist of the handle, two doors opened to receive the new blade. There was the ivory-backed hair-brush, the round brown plastic tobacco-pouch, shaped like a discus. And there was the worn blue-plastic-covered spectacle case, which unpopped and clicked open to reveal his father's glasses, still pinioned at the corner by a bit of fuse-wire in place of a missing screw, the temporary repair that had become permanent.

He put the glasses to one side and dug deeper into the case. His hand felt a small square envelope whose contents were squashy. He drew it out to reveal the old-fashioned pinkish package of a Durex condom.

It moved him strangely. First, he found it sexually arousing. But at the same time it bewildered him, with its implications about his parents' relationship, raising again the incongruous idea of their having had a sex-life, of their making love, of the mystery of his own existence.

And it made him the more determined to carry through his plan for the day.

He had to be at Garrettway for a tutorial at ten o'clock that morning, so when he left the house, he wore his ordinary clothes and carried his father's in a shapeless bag he had kept since school. His plan was to change identity in the gents' lavatories beneath Brighton Station.

There was no problem. The large tiled space was empty when he arrived. He put in a coin and entered one of the cubicles. But he felt sweaty and tense, and his fingers fumbled as he struggled with shirt buttons.

He heard footsteps on the tiled floor, and froze. But there was only the swish of a man peeing and the footsteps receded.

Forcing calmness on himself, he stripped off and started to put on his father's clothes. As he did so, as he became engulfed in their familiar smell, his confidence grew. He was doing the right thing. He felt very together, his concentration suddenly good. He remembered to transfer the money from his own jacket to his father's. He had drawn a hundred pounds out of his Post Office Savings Account. Surely that would be enough, even for a London prostitute. And if the act freed him of the millstone which had been around his neck for years, then it would be cheap at the price.

Changed, and with his own clothes stowed in the bag, he sat for a moment on the lavatory seat to compose himself. A sudden panic hit him as he thought of his mother. What would she have said if she had known what he was planning?

Breathing deeply, he mastered the fear. It had to be done.

He took his father's spectacle-case out of the overcoat pocket, removed the glasses and put them on. The graffiti-scrawled walls around him blurred, and that restored his confidence. It made him feel that people looking at him would receive the same indefinite impression, as though he had assumed a cloak of invisibility.

Carefully flushing the lavatory to maintain an alibi for anybody who might be listening (there was no one), he opened the door and walked out.

He used his normal voice when he bought his ticket, but the man behind the glass did not look at him. Nor did the girl in the bookshop from whom he bought a copy of the *Daily Mirror*. Nor did anyone else, as he walked through the barrier and caught the next train to Victoria.

He walked around Soho for a long time, summoning up courage. He went into sex-shops, secure in his bespectacled invisibility, and in dank booths put 50ps in slots to see brief, blurred scenes of intercourse flicker against the white screens on the doors. He went into peep-shows, where further 50ps opened letter-box traps to reveal bored girls fingering their genitals to crackly music. It all had the desired effect, arousing him till he ached for relief. He grew more and more desperate. He had to do it. It would be all right. God, he needed it.

In his perambulations, he had earmarked the one he was going to. Down a cross-alley off Wardour Street, beside the steel-meshed window of a Topless Bar, was a doorway whose bell-pushes offered 'Mandy—First Floor' and 'Cleo—Second Floor—Walk Up.' He decided that 'Mandy' was going to be the one.

Just before three o'clock closing-time, he went into a pub and downed two large Scotches. He had eaten no lunch and they made him feel disembodied. But they also had the desired effect of making him care less, of convincing him that what he was about to do did not matter.

One more visit to a peep-show restored the desperation of lust. Looking neither to left nor right, he strode along to 'Mandy's' doorway. Without slowing down, he walked in.

Inside, it was surprisingly quiet. His footsteps sounded heavily on the uncarpeted stairs, but he did not falter. He only stopped when he was on the landing.

Here, incongruously, he was reminded of the Garrettway School of Languages. The natural proportions of the landing, like those of Garrettway's hall, had been destroyed by partition walls. The boarded fire-doors were the same. Only the number of bars and padlock-rings showed this to be a venue of a different sort.

A printed card, reading 'Mandy', was drawing-pinned to one of the doors. Too far committed now to stop, he banged against the dark-grey fireproofing.

Simultaneous with his knocking, he heard the click of a latch turning. The door, still secured by a chain, opened about six inches, and through the space a wrinkled face under dyed red hair peered.

'Yes?'

'Mandy?' he asked, shocked by the thought that this might be what was on offer.

'The young lady's busy at the moment,' said the maid. 'Could you come back in ten minutes?'

The door re-closed, and the latch snapped home.

For a moment he stood on the landing,

breathless. Then the clash of reality against his fantasy hit him.

He ran down the stairs, hailed the first empty cab he saw, and told the driver to take him to Victoria.

In the train back to Brighton, he sat mesmerised, careless whether anyone penetrated his disguise. He felt soiled, disgusting, as his mind pitilessly kept superimposing the wizened face with its dyed red locks over the pure image of Madeleine.

8

' "The wandering outlaw of his own dark mind," ' Madeleine quoted, using her fine reading voice for Paul's benefit. 'That's how Childe Harold is described, and it was inevitable, given the kind of reputation the poet had, that Childe Harold should have been identified with Byron.'

Paul nodded. He sat in his usual posture of tutorial discomfort, a copy of Byron's *Complete Works* prudently open on his lap. After the turmoil of the last few days, he felt calmer. He was with Madeleine, and he knew that there could never be any other woman for him. He felt half-drugged, as ever, in her presence.

'It's very difficult for us now to imagine the impact of this poem when it first came out. People in 1812 were just not prepared for a character like Childe Harold. He was a new kind of hero, the first anti-hero, if you like. The first two Cantos made Byron famous overnight.'

'What—just a poem?'

'Ah, you say *just* a poem, but you have to remember there wasn't any television in those days, no radio, no pop records. What Byron offered was all those things rolled into one. Something very new, a bit naughty, a bit shocking, but, above all, profoundly exciting. You can see that, can't you?'

Paul let out a grunt which he hoped implied that he could see it, but in fact, though almost everything else was capable of driving him into a frenzy of excitement, 'Childe Harold's Pilgrimage' left him cold. The memories of the books and videos he had seen excited him; at that moment the sight through thin wool of the depression of her brassière strap in Madeleine's rounded shoulder excited him almost unbearably; but Byron didn't seem to have the same magic.

'You have read it, haven't you?' asked the owner of the brassière strap. 'The first two Cantos, anyway?'

'Oh yes. Most of it. Well, some of it.'

'Even from just a bit of it you must have seen what an original character Byron had created. Here you have a man who has tried everything, indulged himself in every sensual exprience, a man who has "felt the fulness of satiety" . . . you do understand what 'satiety' means, do you Paul?'

'Well, yes. More or less, I think. Not exactly,' he admitted.

'It means sort of fulness . . . *over* fulness, if you like. It means that Childe Harold had tried everything and still not found what it was that would satisfy him, and so he set off on this pilgrimage in search of new experience. He wanted anything new, anything that would stimulate him. To put it in modern terms, he was "living for kicks".'

She was rather taken aback by the blank expression that greeted this phrase. 'I'm sorry. That's probably a very sixties thing to say. What I mean was that Childe Harold was prepared to immerse himself in any experience, to live for the senses, to do anything, regardless of common sense or danger, even if it was self-destructive, so long as he thought it might revive his jaded palate. Do you see what I mean?'

'Yes, I think so. You mean—like glue-sniffing?'

'Glue-sniffing?'

'Well, people who sniff glue just do it for a fix, you know, indulging the senses. And nowadays I suppose Childe Harold would be into glue-sniffing, wouldn't he?'

An expression not unlike a wince traversed Madeleine's forehead. 'All right. If you like. But the interesting thing about Childe Harold is that, even as he courts new experience, he knows that it's not going to satisfy him. But he has to go on, desperately searching for different sensations.' She reassumed the voice that had passed Grade Six Elocution with Merit.

'With pleasure drugg'd he almost long'd for woe,
And e'en for change of scene would seek the shades below.'

Now, that means that he would be prepared even to go down to hell to get some sort of excitement. It was an amazingly self-destructive impulse.'

'They say glue-sniffing's like that, too. People who do it don't really want to go on living.'

The perfect brow wrinkled again. 'Yes, but the thing about Childe Harold—or

104

Byron as we see him through Childe Harold—is that he knows it's all a deception, he knows that no sensation is going to free him of his own innate melancholy. There's a good quote on that.'

She reached for some papers on the table by her side. Paul was painfully aware of the outlined curve of her breast. The hand of his imagination sidled under the back of her pullover, neatly unsnapped the clasp of her brassière then slipped round the front to cradle the sagging warmth. He adjusted the position of Byron's *Complete Works*.

'It's somewhere . . . oh yes, here we are. Listen—this is what Byron wrote: "Why, at the very height of desire and human pleasure—worldly, social, amorous, ambitious, or even avaricious, does there mingle a certain sense of doubt and sorrow—a fear of what is to come—a doubt of what is—a retrospect to the past, leading to a prognostication of the future?" You see, he was recognising the Pain that is at the centre of Pleasure, the closeness of the two things. However deeply he threw himself into experience, he could never lose himself.'

She fixed the violet-blue eyes on Paul. He removed his imagination's hands (both of them got in on the act now) from inside her pullover, blushed and looked away. 'You do see what I'm getting at, don't you, Paul?'

'Yes, I suppose so.' Suddenly he felt flooded with despair. 'What he was saying was it's no good trying to do anything.'

'What do you mean?'

'Well, whatever you do, whatever you want, it's not worth bothering, because if you ever got it—which you probably won't —then you're only going to be disappointed or hurt.'

Madeleine spoke very softly. 'Have you found that, Paul—that everything you want either disappoints you or hurts you?'

He gave a little nod without looking at her. 'Pretty much,' he mumbled.

Madeleine looked at the troubled curve of his head and felt a sudden sense of strength. The poor boy was suffering, and she could help him. She, Madeleine Severn, with all her wealth of maturity, with all her knowledge of life and love, could share some of it with him. She could advise him, just as she had advised her niece, Laura. She could make up for the deficiencies in Paul's parents, just as she had compensated for Aggie's. She could be not just a teacher, but also a friend, expanding her educational role to incorporate the pastoral.

She leant forward towards the boy. 'Listen, Paul, you mustn't think of life like that. Not at your age. For you life should be opening up, it should be an exciting birthday present of opportunities and experiences to be sampled and relished. When you are a bit older . . .' She sighed. 'When you have lived a little more, when you have experienced real disappointment and real hurt, then perhaps you have an excuse for cynicism.' She let a little pause linger wistfully in the air. 'But even those of us who have had our share of suffering have to try not to let cynicism triumph. Even if you have known sadness, you must never believe that all experience will be sad. There are always new things to see, new people to meet, and everything and everyone has something to offer you. You must be open to experience. Remember that bit of Keats I read you—"let us open our leaves like a flower and be passive and receptive. . . ." That's how we all must be in life, ready for anything, hungry for experience.'

Paul dared to look at her. Her face seemed very close. Her perfume surrounded and embalmed him; her eyes seemed to stare into his soul.

'I'm hungry for experience,' he mumbled.

'Good. That's right. At your age you've got to want life. Even at my age,' she added with a little laugh, 'you've got to want life. Even if there has been . . . much sadness in your life, one still must not be frightened. You must challenge life, see what you want and go out and get it. You may be disappointed and hurt, as you say—yes, that's a risk we all run—but you can be wonderfully surprised by joy. And when that happens, suddenly everything else seems all right. You take my word for it. I know.'

Their faces were still very close. Paul was becoming obsessed with the wetness of her lips. Byron's *Complete Works* stirred uneasily on his lap.

'What is the matter?' asked Madeleine intimately. 'Is it a girl?'

He nodded slowly, still the same distance away from her.

'What—you've fallen for someone who doesn't feel the same way about you?'

He nodded again. Their eyes remained locked.

'How do you know she doesn't?'

'Well, it just, you know, seems unlikely. I mean, I doubt if she's ever thought of me in that way. You know, she sort of seems . . . above me.'

Madeleine emitted one of her silvery laughs. Its breeze was warm on Paul's face. 'Oh, you silly boy. So many men seem to think like that, seem to put women on a pedestal, as if they were much more different than they really are. It's strange . . . men are always supposed to be the tough, uncaring sex, and yet, in my experience, I have found them often to be far too sensitive, far too cautious, far less practical than a woman would be in the same circumstances. A lot of men are very soppy, terrible romantics. What you have to remember, Paul . . .' As she spoke, she reached out and took his bruised and swollen hand. Hers was warm and infinitely soft; his own felt to him as wet and twitchy as a landed fish, 'is that women feel for men very much the same as men feel for women. They want love, they feel desire. You mustn't be afraid of them. You say this one you've fallen for is too far above you. Well, that's silly. And it's undervaluing yourself. What do you think's so terrible about you? Be a bit confident. You're an attractive young man. I'm sure there are lots of girls who'd love to go out with you. But you must stop thinking of them as goddesses or idols. They're just girls. . . . You haven't got any sisters, have you?' she asked suddenly.

He shook his head minimally, unwilling to make any move that might break the spell between them. 'Only child,' he murmured.

'That's a pity,' said Madeleine. 'I'm told that nothing so de-mystifies girls for a boy as to have a few sisters. But there were girls at your school and at Sixth Form College, weren't there?'

A tiny nod.

'And I'm sure you didn't think all of them were "above" you. Did you? No, of course not. Well, that's the attitude you must develop towards this one you're in love with now. Treat her like a human being. Talk to her. Tell her what you feel. You've got nothing to lose. The worst she can say is that she doesn't feel the same for you. And who knows—you might get a lovely surprise. You might discover that she's been feeling exactly the same for you ever since she met you and she hasn't had the nerve to put it into words either.'

'Do you really think so?'

Madeleine gave a little smile and showed her perfect teeth. 'It's worth a try, isn't it?'

Paul couldn't believe the way things were turning out. His clammy hand was still lightly held in hers. Her lips were only six inches away from his. 'I suppose it is,' he replied slowly.

Madeleine gave his hand a little shake of encouragement. 'Go on. It's easy. You just have to look her in the eyes and say, "Sharon, I love you." '

'Sharon?' He repeated the name in disbelief.

Madeleine gave a coy smile. 'I've got a good memory, Paul. You introduced me in the pub, remember.' The smile became knowing. 'And I could see then that you were absolutely over the moon about her. You looked goggle-eyed. I've never seen anyone so smitten.'

'But that wasn't—'

'Don't deny it.' She shook his hand from side to side, playfully.

'But I—'

'Looked to me remarkably like an expression of love.'

111

He decided to take the risk. 'Yes, all right. It was an expression of love. But what you don't realise is—'

Whether he would ever have made the revelation he intended, and how she would have reacted to it, were questions that would never be answered. At that moment there was a little tap on the door and it opened to admit Bernard Hopkins.

Madeleine looked up at his entrance and let go of Paul's hand. This was not done with any guilt or embarrassment; she simply discarded it. Paul remained frozen in midsentence, crouched on the edge of his chair.

'Just your schedule for next week,' said Bernard's voice behind him. 'I was up in Julian's office and saw it there and since I was passing. . . .'

'Oh, thank you.' Madeleine stretched out the hand that had so recently held Paul's and took the envelope.

'Well, cheerio,' Paul heard Bernard say. But he didn't see the older man mouth, 'Six-thirty', before he left the room. He did, however, see Madeleine's acknowledgement of the assignation, which took the form of a quick wink, and which filled Paul with black, unreasoning fury.

Her pupil did not say much more as Madeleine completed the tutorial and set him some Shelley to read before their next meeting. He left with only the most perfunctory goodbye, his eyes dark and preoccupied.

Madeleine sat still for a moment before she gathered up her books and papers. She felt pleased with her morning's work. She had really got through to the boy on a personal level, she had really helped him. It was a good feeling to know that one was doing something important for someone else.

Through her spread the warm glow that always came as, unwittingly, with infinite care and solicitude, she cut her dainty swathe through everyone who came into contact with her.

Paul's chameleon mood had settled now to black hatred, and the hatred was fixed on Bernard Hopkins. The hatred born of the fact that the man was seeing Madeleine had now been compounded by his interruption of Paul's declaration. Paul had felt so confident at that moment; he had felt confident even that Madeleine had been joking about

Sharon, teasing, knowing that she herself was the real object of his affections.

And then Bernard Hopkins had come in and spoiled it.

Paul was too angry to suffer the confinement of the bus, so he walked home. At least home was his ultimate destination, but he walked by a circuitous route, glaring truculently into shop windows, reading into everything he saw some criticism, some stricture on his own failure.

It was in a shop in one of the shabby roads that run down from Brighton Station. The shop sold Army Surplus goods, camouflage jackets, billycans, rucksacks, boots and suchlike.

And knives.

The one that caught his eye was a sheath-knife with a black handle.

He went into the shop and bought it.

His mother was out at work when he got back to the house. He went straight up to his bedroom and fixed the sheath-knife on to his belt. Facing the large mirror on the wall, he suddenly whipped the blade out of the sheath and slashed at the space before him.

He snarled into the mirror and felt strong.

He made a few more exploratory jabs and slashes.

Then, very calmly, he rolled up the sleeves of his pullover and shirt, baring his forearm. He inspected the exposed flesh. He had no wish to cut a vein. This was to be no gesture of escapism or defeat. It was a gesture of strength.

He set the point of the new blade against the skin and, with a quick, steady movement, drew it across.

At first there was just a white line. Then, slowly, bubbles of blood welled up and joined until there was a red line. Slowly, this began to trickle down towards his hand.

Paul went into the bathroom to wash the wound in cold water. And on the face that stared back at him from the mirror over the basin was a look of triumph.

9

In her choice of clothes Madeleine Severn did not follow current fashion, though people who liked her had always said that she had style. She favoured a 'natural' look, avoiding man-made fibres and angularities of cut. For her working days, in the same way that she put her hair up to express a kind of benign efficiency, so she selected a variety of skirts and jumpers which looked businesslike but retained fuzzy, tactile outlines. She avoided bright colours and defined patterns, preferring subtler half-tones and designs whose contours melted together.

When she was not at work, she went for garments that moved around a lot. She liked flowing skirts and hanging sleeves, either in faded pastel colours or smudged Indian prints. She wore many gratuitous shawls and scarves. The style, though personalised, was full of echoes of the sixties, and indeed it

116

had been while she was at Oxford that she had first adopted it.

For the first time she was to entertain Bernard Hopkins in her own home, Madeleine dressed with care. Her tutorial with Paul in the morning had been her only work commitment that day, so she had plenty of time to plan her effects, plenty of time also to prepare the 'light supper' she had offered her guest. After considerable thought, she selected a flowing full-length Indian dress whose tiny design of black on brown blurred into an impression of russet, which she knew would set off the red-gold hair, to be worn that evening deliberately loose, punctiliously dishevelled. It would be the first time Bernard had seen her hair down, and she did not want him to lose any of the impact.

Over her simple peasant robe she draped a fine cream wool shawl, carelessly pinned at the front with a circular silver brooch, rather in the manner of Flora Macdonald. A pair of beige leather clogs completed the ensemble.

Madeleine Severn did not wear make-up, wishing to face the world as herself and confident of the excellence of her complexion. When nature had chosen so skilfully to complement her hair with her skin, it seemed perverse to upset the balance. She did however use a cleansing-lotion made from natural ingredients (largely rose-water) and maintained the perfection of her teeth by rigorous brushing and flossing. A dab of the perfume which had had such an effect on Paul (again a subtle distillation of the aroma of flowers) was then applied behind each ear and to the inside of each wrist. Madeleine Severn's appearance was complete.

She moved on to the promised 'light supper'. A soufflé, she had decided, would be an appropriate demonstration of the breadth of her skills. Haddock, she thought. Folding in the egg whites, of course, would have to be done at the last minute, but she made the béchamel sauce, adding the egg yolks and flaked fish. Then she turned her attention to a little selection of unexpected salads. Mozzarella and orange. Watercress, celery and walnut. Flageolets and fennel. She put the bottle of Liebfraumilch she had bought into the fridge.

By half-past five all these preparations had been made, and she turned her attention to the tiny sitting-room. The pile of cushions

118

on the low sofa did not look sufficiently random, so she disarrayed them with care. She draped a beaded shawl artlessly over the back of her old rocking-chair. She opened the *Guardian*, which she had not had time to look at that day, at the Features page, folded it back on itself and laid it asymmetrically on the low pine coffee-table. She inspected her bookshelves and, finding the spines too parallel, leant a few this way and that, took out others and replaced them horizontally on top. She extracted a Penguin edition of Swinburne, opened it at 'A Forsaken Garden', and laid it, text down, on the floor by the sofa, as if it had just been abandoned there at the sound of the door-bell.

She went across to the record-player. This was an old Dansette she had bought while at university. Though she could easily have afforded a more modern set-up, she stuck with calculated eccentricity to the outmoded mono machine. Most of the records dated from the same period. Some of the pop ones, her copy of *Sergeant Pepper's Lonely Hearts Club Band*, her two Mamas and Papas LPs, were crackly with over-use. But she went on playing them. There had been few additions to her collection since Oxford. She bought Leonard Cohen and still, in mournful moods, wallowed in his pretension. Joni Mitchell, too. And a Billy Holliday reissue. But that, the most recent purchase, had been bought over ten years before.

For Bernard, though, she didn't think pop music was right. He was that much older, seemed perhaps a little too serious for the Mamas and the Papas. She realised, with a little spurt of excitement, that she did not yet know him well enough to be able to gauge his tastes. She just felt confident that there would be time, that they would get to know each other, that they were embarking on more than a brief relationship.

Vivaldi's *Four Seasons* seemed bright enough, tasteful, and safe. She slipped the worn LP out of its sleeve, and put it on the turntable. Just as the music started, the telephone rang.

She switched the record-player off and went across to answer the ringing. She felt sure it would Bernard. He would be calling perhaps to say he'd been delayed, that he would be a little late. She wasn't worried. She knew he would come.

It wasn't Bernard. It was her niece, Laura.

'Laura, how lovely. Seems ages since I've seen you.'

'I know. Been busy.' But it was said amicably, not with that new, rather upsetting, tone that had been creeping into Laura's conversations with her aunt recently.

'Everything going well? I gather from Aggie there's a new boyfriend on the scene.'

'Yes.'

'And that's going well?'

'Pretty well, I think,' Laura replied cautiously. Then suddenly she said, 'I'd like to see you, Madeleine. Have a talk.'

'Of course.' Madeleine was all warmth. She had known the estrangement would only be temporary. She had known that Laura would soon come back to her, would soon need her womanly advice. 'What, a lunch?'

Laura worked in Brighton and, until recently, the two of them had met fairly regularly at lunchtime.

'Yes, that'd be fine. Any day, really, from my point of view.'

'Well, let me think. How am I placed for classes?' Madeleine made some play of consulting an imaginary diary. 'Thursday. Thursday be all right?'

'Fine.'

'Look forward to seeing you then. Usual time? Usual place?'

The usual time was a quarter to one. The usual place was a health-food shop in the Lanes which had a small restaurant area behind.

'OK,' said Laura.

Madeleine was filled with satisfaction as she put the phone down. It was such a good feeling, helping people. In the morning she had been able to give so much to the young boy, Paul, and now Laura was coming back with her problems. Because, in spite of the insouciance of her niece's manner, Madeleine had no doubt that the girl had some sort of problem, one that she needed to share with someone of her own sex, someone with a little more knowledge of the world.

At that moment the doorbell rang. Madeleine restarted the Vivaldi and gave the room one final look. The reproduction of Millais' *The Bridesmaid* over the fireplace was too aggressively straight. She nudged the frame at the bottom to set it slightly askew.

Inspired, she took the string of black mourning-beads that hung from the mirror and draped them over the corner of the picture. It was the little touches, she knew, that counted.

Then she went to answer the door.

Bernard was properly appreciative of the soufflé, but he did not eat a great deal of it. He felt remarkably nervous, alone with Madeleine. It was a long time since he had been in this sort of situation with a woman and he would no doubt take a while to adjust. At the moment he felt as jumpy as he had in his late teens when he had made his first stumbling attempts at forming relationships with girls.

In those days his worries had been mainly about whether he felt enough for them, but this time he had no doubts about his feelings for Madeleine. He wondered if he had ever been so preoccupied with one person, so blinkered to the rest of the world. But, in spite of his certainty, the nervousness remained. He toyed gamely with his mozzarella and orange salad.

'More wine?' asked Madeleine, profferring the Liebfraumilch.

Bernard put his hand warily over his glass. 'Perhaps I'd better not. Still got my Turk to see at nine. Must be coherent. Wouldn't do for him to go back to Turkey imagining conversational English is all slurred and garbled.'

Madeleine laughed, gently raised his fingers and poured wine into the glass. 'You'll be all right. From what you say of his aptitude, even getting Mr Nassiri to speak *drunken* English will be quite an achievement.'

Bernard turned his hand, and hers nestled into it. His brown eyes looked into her violet-blue ones. 'Oh, Madeleine,' he said, in a voice tinged with resignation. 'Madeleine, Madeleine.'

She smiled at him serenely.

'Oh, Madeleine, what am I going to do about you?'

'Keep seeing me, I hope.'

He nodded ruefully, in a way that was both troubled and at the same time seemed to mock its trouble. 'Yes. I'm afraid we have no alternative.'

She pouted. 'You sound as if you wish you did have an alternative.'

'No. I don't. It's just. . . .' He sighed. 'If

only things were always as straightforward as they seem to be at this moment.'

'I don't understand.'

'I mean that while we're here together, everything seems logical and simple. But as soon as we're apart, everything else will crowd in, all the problems, all the things that are difficult, all the things that don't work, that don't fit.'

'Are you talking about your wife?'

He shook his head abruptly, almost in exasperation. 'No, I'm not talking about my wife. My wife's irrelevant. She doesn't exist as far as you're concerned. I wish I'd never mentioned her to you.'

'You didn't, actually. I heard about her from the Eyes and Ears of Garrettway, Stella Franklin. But I would have found out anyway. You couldn't have kept it from me.'

'I don't know. With you I wanted a new start. I didn't want there to be any lies between us, just honesty, so that our relationship could grow, without being . . . sort of . . . pressured.'

'Saying you hadn't got a wife,' Madeleine rebuked gently 'would hardly have been honest, would it?'

'But we could have. . . .' He abandoned

the idea with a sad shake of his head. 'No. I've got myself locked into this situation now.' He shrugged, then brightened. 'So you were asking Stella about me?'

'As soon as I saw you, I wanted to know everything about you.'

'I had the same problem with you.' He sighed. 'Yes, I'm afraid we both seem to have got it.' His tone implied that 'it' was not necessarily a very desirable thing to have.

Madeleine shook his hand from side to side in gentle admonition. 'Don't sound so gloomy. It'll be all right.'

'Do you think so?'

'Of course. If something's meant to happen, it happens. The right thing happens.'

'It hasn't in the past,' he said dully.

She was stung. 'You mean you've been in this situation lots of times?'

'No,' he said wearily. 'Just life generally. Things don't always work out—don't seem to work out for me, perhaps I should say.' He felt very close to her. He wanted to say more, to confide his real meaning, but something held him back.

'You mean your Shirley?' asked Madeleine.

Again he denied it, but she did not take any notice. 'No, it must have been terrible for you. To have had a love that worked and that is then destroyed, not by any infidelity or loss of passion, but by something external, something over which you have no control.'

He felt too tired to correct her view of his situation. She knew nothing about it, and he knew that, for him to keep her, she would probably have to remain in ignorance.

'You must feel terribly guilty,' she said softly.

He nodded. That at least was true.

'But you shouldn't, really. It's not your fault. It's just your misfortune. And, Bernard, whatever happens with us, we will be discreet. She'll never find out, I promise.'

He looked away.

'I have moments of guilt, too. I told you about John. John Kaczmarek. The one who died. I told you. And I never thought that I would ever feel anything for anyone else comparable to what I felt for him. Now I feel a little guilty, as if in some way I've let him down.'

Her brow furrowed, as with emotion. In fact, it was furrowing as she tried to summon up the image of John Kaczmarek. She had increasing difficulty these days in remembering exactly what he had looked like, and had constantly to consult the few photographs she had kept of him. But they proved inadequate prompts, their colours now subtly false, his expressions unlike the expressions she remembered. John Kaczmarek had become just a feeling in her mind, a memory of something important that had once happened to her, that had shaped her character, but whose details remained obstinately imprecise.

'Guilt and sex,' Bernard observed with resignation, 'seem to go together.'

Madeleine tossed her head in exasperation at this fact. Her red-gold hair rippled, just as it was meant to. 'I'm sure it's only in this country that we react like that. Or at least this country's worse than most. Primitive societies don't have these hang-ups,' she generalised blithely. 'Oh, I long sometimes just to be simple and primitive. I'm sure if we took away all the trappings of society and convention, if people could just get together as people, everything would work so much better.'

'I know what you mean,' Bernard agreed.

'I think that about you.'

'About me? I don't understand.'

'I'd like to be with you somewhere that's out of time, somewhere that's peaceful, that's cut off from the rest of the world, away from memories of the past and fears of the future, somewhere where there could just be the two of us, insulated from everything else.'

He feared that the speech sounded corny. He had never had any problem with words, shaping them into lines and sequences of lines, but he had never been a good judge of their impact. What he had said to Madeleine was more or less what he meant, but he was afraid that the words might sound false to her.

He need not have worried. Madeleine loved words for their own sake, loved people to be articulate and, particularly, loved people to talk in abstract rather than specific terms.

'Maybe we'll get that privacy we want one day, Bernard,' she said. And she leant down to bestow a chaste kiss on his forehead.

He looked at his watch. 'I'm afraid I must be on my way. Got to get to see my friend at the Metropole.'

He was in fact not sorry that the encounter was about to end. Partly this arose from the delicious confidence that they would meet again soon, but also there was a braking instinct within him, that didn't want things to move too fast, to get out of hand. Already he was worried that too much had been said that evening, that too much had been committed. He felt guilt and a little fear. He was so determined that the mistakes of the past should not repeat themselves. This time no one must get hurt. So he needed solitude, time on his own to think about what was happening, to assimilate and assess the new situation in which he found himself.

Madeleine, too, was not displeased that he had to go. She had known the time-limit of the evening from the start and she was a great believer in the rationing of romance. Life, she thought, should be made up of wonderful moments and little quiet times day-dreaming about those moments and building on the day-dreams. The 'light supper' with Bernard had stocked her up with some days' supply of fantasy-fodder, and that was all that she had required of it. She, like him, was aware that their relationship could not stand still, but she, like him, was in no violent rush to move on to the next stage.

She stood behind him in the tiny hall as he put on his coat. Then he turned to face her.

'Thank you for the supper. It was really lovely. Just what was needed.' He swayed in front of her, uncertain.

'And we'll see each other again soon.'

'Of course. Round the Garrettway or. . . .' He gave a little smile and shrugged.

'Yes. I was thinking, Bernard. . . .'

'Hmm?'

'We must play it very cool at the Garrettway. Stella is so nosey, such a gossip. And I wouldn't put a lot of money on Julian's discretion. Probably better if we try not to take too much notice of each other there. You know, just colleagues. You can ring me here if you want to fix anything.'

'If you like. Though it doesn't seem necessary to. . . .'

'I'm thinking of Shirley, Bernard.'

He nodded, put in his place. She's much more concerned to keep it from my wife than I am, he thought ironically.

'I'd better be off. Mr Nassiri waits.'

'Yes.' Madeleine leant forward to place a kiss on his cheek. His face moved round suddenly and their lips fused. Arms found their way around the two bodies, and they pressed fiercely against each other, moulding together the contours of flesh as if their clothes had not been there.

It was a long, hungry, searching kiss and, when they finally drew apart, both looked a little shocked by its violence, almost shy at the new facets of their personalities so suddenly exposed.

'Oh God,' Bernard murmured huskily, 'I want you.'

'I want you too,' Madeleine's words came out instinctively and what she had said gave her a new sense of shock. But she knew that she meant it.

'Well,' Bernard pronounced with grim resolution, 'we must see what we can do about that.'

And, still shaken by the strength of the lust he felt, he went off to teach Mr Nassiri conversational English.

10

On the evening that Madeleine entertained
Bernard to haddock soufflé and a variety of
interesting salads, Sharon Wilkinson went
to the cinema with Tony Ashton. He had
rung out of the blue suggesting that they
should go out together, and she had been
unable to think of any particular reason to
refuse. After the way Paul Grigson had behaved on their last date, she felt she owed
no special loyalty in that direction.

Besides, Tony Ashton was quite attractive
and rather intriguing. True, he wore an ear-
ring, which was something of which Sharon's father (and so automatically Sharon
herself) disapproved strongly. Also, he didn't
have a job, so his score wasn't very high on
the husband/mortgage/fitted kitchen/match-
ing bathroom suite scale. But a friend who
worked with her at Boots had been out with
him a few times and had said that he was

a very good dancer. This gave him an immediate appeal, offering Sharon wonderful images of fun at the local discos. She was therefore a little disappointed when Tony, on picking her up at the agreed time, announced that they were going to the cinema. But she did not say anything. After all, at least on the first date, it was the feller's decision what they should do.

Her friend at Boots had also advised her to beware of Tony's wandering hands and, as soon as the lights in the cinema went down, she was made aware of the reasons for this warning. His left arm was immediately around her shoulders, which was perhaps not unusual, but his right hand was equally immediately on her right breast, kneading away through the cardigan, blouse and brassière—and that was. She might have expected some approach of that sort halfway through the main feature, but to encounter it during the trailer for 'NEXT PRESENTATION AT THIS CINEMA' seemed distinctly premature. She removed the hand firmly from her breast and placed it down on Tony's lap.

This was a bad idea. Turning his hand and clasping hers, he pressed it against somewhere totally unsuitable. Sharon snatched her hand away and, folding her arms rigidly over her breasts, watched the screen.

Her point seemed to have been made, because Tony sat back demurely through the rest of the trailers and advertisements, until the cinema's management deemed that their customers had earned an intermission and flashed up pictures of soft drinks, ice-cream and hot dogs, available variously from the sales staff and in the foyer. Tony asked if Sharon would care for any of these delicacies and, on receiving the answer that she wouldn't mind a Coke, went chivalrously off to the foyer to furnish her with one. On his way back, slightly less chivalrously, he topped up the cardboard cup from a quarter-bottle of vodka he had in his pocket.

Sharon thanked him for the drink and commented that it tasted a bit funny. Tony was of the opinion that this was probably caused by the water which had been used to make the ice.

The lights then dimmed for the main feature. It was not the sort of romantic story which Sharon favoured. Instead it was one of those farragos about American college students, in which the crudeness of the action is matched by the crudeness of the dialogue, and titillation provided by much peering into locker-rooms, groping in the back of cars and nude bathing.

Tony, clearly aware of the film's content, took the opening credits as a cue to recommence his assault on Sharon. The wandering hands, of which she had been warned, were instantly all over her, pressing, squeezing, tickling, kneading. At the same time Tony's lips were brought in as reinforcements. They moved first to nibble her ear, then, parting, they released a tongue to probe its orifice. This produced in her a sensation of tickling, but had no other effect.

Her jaw was then moved round and his lips fused with hers. She returned the kisses. They were, after all, what was expected. Boys asked girls out because they wanted to kiss them, and it would have been churlish of her to refuse this harmless interchange.

What the hands were doing, on the other hand, was not what, to Sharon's mind, boys asked girls out for. At least, it might be the reason for the invitation, but it was not a liberty that she thought proper to grant. As with most areas of her life, Sharon had very strict ground-rules about her body, about which bits were available, to whom and under what circumstances. These ground-rules came down to two basic prohibitions: nothing was allowed to go on inside her clothes, and nothing was allowed to go on below her waist.

But Tony Ashton's assault was so pertinacious that Sharon realised that if she did not wish to resort to unpleasantness (and she didn't think the moment for unpleasantness had come quite yet), she might have to make some adjustments to her ground-rules. One or other of the prohibitions would have to be relaxed. It did not take her long to decide which. Hands on the flesh of her upper torso could be tolerated, but incursions below the boundary of her waistband could not.

These negotiations and trade-offs were conducted without words, but Sharon managed to make her terms perfectly clear. She deterred the downward movement of the hands by wriggling so violently each time they threatened, that cinema-goers in nearby seats turned to see what was going on. The use of this ploy on three occasions was sufficient to embarrass even Tony Ashton, and the hands moved up out of the prohibited zone.

Once above the safety margin, they encountered less resistance in their probes through cardigan and blouse-buttons to the warm flesh beneath. They were not even slapped off when the right one undid two of the buttons and sidled in to circle a brassièred breast. Nor was there adverse reaction when the same pioneer insinuated itself between nylon and skin to encapsulate the breast itself. Emboldened by its partner's success, the other made a flanking movement from the other side of the blouse up to the clasp of the brassière and, with an expert squeezing pressure, released it.

The right hand, now given more room to manoeuvre, found the small pimple of a nipple with its thumb and forefinger and started a gentle cigarette-rolling motion.

Sharon, on whom this manoeuvre had been frequently attempted but always before frustrated, was surprised by it. Surprised first that it was happening, and surprised second by the effect its happening had on her. Because, although the stimulation produced a localised tingling, its effects were by no means confined to that part of her body. Other muscles twitched, other parts grew warm and melted. When Tony, while maintaining this stimulation, kissed her, the kisses seemed to have a new potency, linking together the separate sensations into something which washed through her whole body and whose intensity she found a little frightening.

As the film reached the final freeze of its clumsy dénouement and the credits started to roll, Tony removed his right hand from its occupation and Sharon almost found herself regretting its departure.

The cinema-goers shambled to their feet and Tony's hands reached chastely to find his jacket beneath the seat. Sharon, confused and blushing, reached under her blouse and, with difficulty, reattached the errant straps of her brassière. When she stood up, Tony gave her a sardonic sideways smile and, placing two fingertips on her shoulder, led her out of the cinema.

Of course he wanted to come in for a coffee when they got back to her house. It was about ten to eleven. On a weekday her parents were unlikely to have finished clearing up in the restaurant till midnight at the earliest, so they certainly couldn't be expected home before half-past. An hour and forty minutes to survive.

He clasped her to him and kissed her deeply as soon as they were in the hall. Sharon was very aware of the contours of his body against her, and also of the way her body was responding to them.

She broke loose, straightened her clothes and in a voice of convention said, 'Won't you come in and sit down?'

He gave her another sideways smile as he slouched through into the sitting-room. Ignoring the three easychairs, he slumped down on the sofa. Sharon hovered in the doorway. 'I'll just go and put the kettle on.'

'Sod coffee.' As he spoke, he reached out for her hand and pulled her down on top of him. She felt helpless as he pressed her to him, his hands roaming, pulling up her blouse at the back, reaching, probing, invading.

His tongue, too, was making its own incursions, stifling her complaints as it probed into her mouth. Then it moved downwards, licking from the point of her chin, over the skin of her neck, down to the cleft between her breasts. She felt the cold metal of his ear-ring against her flesh. Then her blouse-buttons were somehow undone, her brassière unclasped, and his tongue was continuing the stimulation that his fingers had started in the cinema.

She felt those fingers now, worrying at the zip at the back of her skirt. Something gave and all at once they were inside, pressing her crutch hard against his.

'No!' She drew back, prised herself off him, stood upright, one hand salvaging her tumbled skirt, the other trying to close the front of her blouse.

Tony looked up at her with a lazy grin. 'You don't mean no.'

'I do. I do.'

'No. I can tell. You're panting for it. I'll give you a good time. Come here.' He reached out a confident hand.

'No, Tony. I can't. I mustn't.'

'Why not? Look here, Sharon, you've been giving me the come-on all evening.'

This didn't seem to her to be true, but she couldn't muster the arguments to deny it. 'I won't.'

'Come on. It's not such a big deal. Don't pretend you haven't done it before.'

'I haven't.'

'Ha, bloody ha. What about laughing boy? What about that little wimp Paul Grigson? Go on, you've put out for him. I'll give you a better time than that.'

Sharon shook her head. There were tears now in her eyes. 'I haven't. Paul and I never. . . . He never has, I'm sure . . . nor have I—really—not with anyone.'

Tony laughed. It was a brisk, unattractive sound.

'And,' she continued defiantly, 'I certainly wouldn't want to do it with you.'

Tony swung his legs round on to the floor and looked at her. He was angry, and he knew he could have her if he wanted to. He was strong enough.

But a virgin. . . . A weeping virgin at that. He wasn't sure that he fancied it.

He rose to his feet. Sharon flinched away from him, fearing a blow. But he just said, 'Goodnight' lightly, and walked to the front door. He still felt angry as he walked home, but not that angry. He'd give Tracey Ruskin a call the next day. No point in going for things that were difficult when you could get them easy.

Sharon felt huge relief when he had gone. She rebuttoned and rezipped her clothes before taking them off and having her customary bath. It had been a narrow escape.

But she didn't feel the satisfaction of virtue triumphant. She felt ill-at-ease as she donned her crisp little nightdress and got into her crisp little bed. She found she could not concentrate on her newest Mills and Boon and, when she turned the light out, sleep did not bring its usual, immediate benison.

She couldn't pretend. She knew what was troubling her. When she had said she did not want to do it with Tony, she had been lying.

Paul Grigson was trying without marked success to keep his mind on Shelley the next morning, when at about half-past eleven his mother came through the front door. He looked up, surprised. Her face was once again drawn and grey.

'You all right?' he asked.

She nodded wryly. 'Oh yes, fine. Well, fine-ish.' She sighed. 'Let us say that the doctor cannot diagnose anything wrong with me.'

'You've just been to the doctor?'

Another nod. 'Yes. Thought I should

check with a so-called expert. But—surprise, surprise—he didn't know. I'm not sure why we bother going to doctors. Either they just admit they don't know or, if they're feeling really adventurous, they diagnose a virus.'

'Well, if he couldn't find anything, you're probably OK.'

But Mrs Grigson wasn't going to be comforted that easily. With a look of pity for Paul's acceptance of such a simplistic solution, she announced, 'He wants me to go into hospital to have some tests.'

The panic thought of his mother's dying again swept through him, but only briefly. 'When?'

'Thursday. That's the next time they've got a bed free. Should be out by the weekend.'

Paul dared to ask what the tests were for.

'Oh God,' his mother sighed dramatically. 'You don't think they tell you *that*.' She became brisk and practical. 'At least it gives me a couple of days to stock up for you. You'll have to cope on your own. Do you think you're capable?'

She couldn't resist that last dig. Paul didn't rise to anger, as she had hoped, but assured her that he could manage.

'I'd better get to work,' his mother said wearily. 'Late enough already.' And slowly, not allowing her son to be unaware of her invalid state, she started to collect her things together.

Paul felt a spasm of guilt, as had been intended, but it did not last. A new thought was blossoming in his mind. He would have the house to himself. For two blissful days he would be on his own, free to invite anyone 'back to my place'.

One of his fantasies of Madeleine instantly shifted location. It moved away from imagined hotels and hillsides to the specific setting of his bedroom.

Julian Garrett was reaching the end of his third afternoon tutorial in a fortnight with the young housewife in Hove, and deciding that he had probably achieved as much as he was likely to for her progress. But she clasped her arms round him as he tried to put his trousers back on.

'Julian, I wish we could have longer together. It's always so rushed. We don't have time to talk.'

'No,' he agreed. 'Well, it's difficult. You've got the kids, your husband.'

145

'He works away a lot. I could unload the kids on to friends for a night. We could spend a whole night together.'

Julian rose from the bed to button up his Turnbull and Asser shirt. 'What you forget, my dear, is that while your family can be so conveniently abandoned, my wife is likely to prove less accommodating.'

'What's she like?' asked the housewife.

'I don't think there's anything to be gained from my answering that question. It's not relevant to any relationship you and I may have.'

'But I feel awful when you're not here. It's terrible trying to pretend with my husband, when all I really want is to be with you.'

'I'm sure you will manage.'

'If only I could make contact when I need to talk to you.'

'I've told you about the situation with my wife. You can't possibly ring me at home, I'm afraid.' He felt increasingly glad that he had fabricated a spouse for this particular encounter; the housewife promised to be very clinging, given the opportunity.

'Surely I can ring you at the school.'

He shook his head. 'My secretary is the

nosiest woman I have ever encountered. She's a widow who fills the emptiness of her life by creating romances for everyone she meets. You can ring me at the school only if you want to put me out of business.'

'Well, it's just so. . . . When you love someone, you want to be with them all the time.'

She was nearing post-coital tears. Julian briskly put on his jacket, straightened his almost-regimental tie and smoothed his hair back in the bedroom mirror. Then he made for the door.

'I'll ring you,' he lied.

Madeleine lay in a hot bath on the Thursday evening, feeling satisfied with her day. She had washed her red-gold hair, which once again fanned out in the water, a detail from Millais' *Ophelia*. She raised one delicate toe and pushed the tap for an infusion of hot water.

She had had her lunch with Laura and, as anticipated, Laura had wanted to talk. Her aunt could see this as soon as the girl walked into the health-food restaurant. Laura was thin, excessively thin for Madeleine's tastes. Madeleine reckoned a certain opulence of line was a prerequisite of feminine beauty. Nor would she have accentuated the angularity with the loosely-hanging, garishly-striped T-shirt dress that Laura had chosen. The hair, too, could have been shown to better advantage. It was reddish, not of course of the same splendour as Madeleine's, more of an auburn, really, but not an unattractive colour. The short, lop-sided cut did not do a great deal for it, though. And no one, surely, could think that those silver ear-rings dangling from a row of perforations were actually attractive. . . . Still, Laura was young. It would take her a few years to develop her own style, Madeleine reflected indulgently.

She felt great warmth for her niece as they embraced. It was good for them to be together again. There was a reassuring furrow on Laura's brow which denoted a problem and which promised confidences.

Laura's problem, it soon became clear, was love, and Madeleine, her past experience of the subject now intensified by the new feelings for Bernard that were growing within her, felt more than competent to offer advice.

Laura's problem, for once, though, was

not unrequited love. The man involved, Terry, apparently felt for her on exactly the same scale as she felt for him. The problem was one of parental opposition, strong opposition from Aggie.

As the situation was unfolded to her, Madeleine glowed. This was her kind of scene, one at which she knew she excelled.

Quickly, she dramatised it in her mind into a Romeo and Juliet scenario, with Aggie cast as both Montagus and Capulets. Laura and Terry became the 'star-cross'd lovers' and she, Madeleine Severn, would have to take the part of a benign Friar Laurence.

'Mum's being an absolute pig about it,' Laura had said, as they settled down with their bean-sprout and kidneybean salads, their grainy wholemeal bread and their carrot juice.

'She doesn't like him?'

'Certainly the impression she's giving.'

'What about Keith?'

Laura shrugged. 'Keith doesn't have a mind of his own. He thinks whatever Mum thinks.'

Madeleine gave a pained nod. 'Yes. I'm afraid I never could quite fathom that relationship. I know I shouldn't say it about your mother, but I just do not understand what she sees in him.'

Laura gave a wry grin. 'Sex. Pure and simple. Nothing more than that. God, you should try living in the house with them. Bloody embarrassing. They're at it all the time.'

Madeleine curled her lip. 'Well, yes, I can see that that would be part of it, but surely not enough to. . . .' She caught Laura's curious expression, and retreated quickly. She did not wish to appear ignorant of the powers of sex. And the unaccustomed feelings that Bernard had aroused made her wonder whether perhaps in the past she had underestimated its influence. 'No, I suppose you're right,' she conceded. 'There's no explaining physical attraction.'

'No, and that's what makes Mum's behaviour to me over Terry so bloody annoying. Bloody hypocritical, in fact.'

'What do you mean?'

'Well, Terry and me. . . .' Laura blushed prettily. In spite of her surface poise, she was still only seventeen, and not a very worldly-wise seventeen. 'I mean, ours is a physical relationship, too.'

'You mean you've slept together?'

'Sure.' The word was meant to sound casual and defiant, but Laura still coloured as she said it.

'Does Aggie know?'

'I haven't actually told her, but she must be bloody stupid if she can't work it out for herself.'

'Is Terry older than you?'

Laura nodded. 'Twenty-six.'

'Married?'

'Separated. You see, he's working down here in Brighton on a building project. He's an architect. So he's only here weekdays, and he's staying in this guest-house, and there's no way he can take me back there, so we're—'

Madeleine interrupted. 'Where does he go at weekends?'

'Back to Hereford. He's still got a house there.'

'Are you sure he hasn't still got a wife there?'

'She may live there, but I told you they're separated.'

'Then why does he go back every weekend?'

'His mother. She's in a nursing-home. Getting very frail now. He feels he must see her whenever he can. Doesn't think she'll be around for very much longer.'

'Hmm. And Aggie won't have him in the house?'

Laura's head shook impatiently. 'It's not that. On the couple of occasions they've met, she's been more or less civil to him. That's not the problem. It's just that whenever I mention the idea of me staying away for a night, she thinks I'm planning to spend it with him and she goes off the deep end.'

'And are you planning to spend these nights with him?'

'Of course I am,' said Laura defiantly. 'I've got to. I need to. It's hopeless. We're in love, he's twenty-six, I'm over sixteen, and so far our sex-life has been limited to the back of his car and the golf-course. Well, I don't know if you've ever conducted an affair like that, but you take my word for it, it's not ideal.'

Madeleine gave a wise, experienced smile. 'I've been lucky. Never been reduced to those sort of expedients.' She moved into her shrewd-observer-of-human-psychology mode. 'Of course, you know why Aggie's behaving like this to you?'

Laura shrugged.

'It's because of what happened to her. You're a constant reminder of where she went wrong, and she's afraid of history repeating itself. You're seventeen, exactly the same age that she was when she . . . made her little mistake. That's why she's overreacting.'

'OK,' said Laura contemptuously, 'I can see that. But she can't think that I'm as naïve a little twit as she was at the same age.' Another blush. 'Terry's not the first man I've slept with. I am on the pill.'

'Have you told Aggie that?'

Laura shook her head, ashamed.

'I see your problem,' Madeleine summed up. 'Don't worry. I'm sure it will sort itself out. Give Aggie a bit of time to get used to the idea that you're grown up and responsible for your actions. And if it's the real thing with Terry, I'm sure it'll survive these difficulties. It may sound a cliché, but love usually does find a way.'

Madeleine's recognition of the cliché didn't make it any less of a cliché, and it didn't satisfy Laura. 'That's not good enough for me, Madeleine. I don't want to know that love will find a way—I want to know the exact way that love is going to find.'

'Well, I suppose you could just ignore Aggie and get Terry to move in somewhere where you can be together without problems.'

'We've been through that. His company's paying for where he is at the moment. He can't afford to go anywhere else. And I can't afford to move out of home—otherwise I'd pack my bags and be in a flat tomorrow.'

Madeleine smiled with a touch of pity and a touch of mockery. 'Then it looks as if you're just going to have to grin and bear it for the time being. At least it's a good test of your love for each other.'

'We don't want our love bloody tested!' snapped Laura. 'We want it expressed. And not just in secret. Have you any idea how cold it is on the golf-course this time of year?'

Madeleine gave a little laugh. 'I sympathise, Laura, but I don't really see how I can help.'

'But you *can*.' The girl was suddenly insistent. 'You can help us. That's why I wanted to see you.'

Madeleine looked puzzled.

'Look, you know how I used to come and stay with you, down in your house. . . ?'

'Yes. You haven't done it so much recently, I may say.' Madeleine could not resist this expression of pique.

'I know, but Mum still wouldn't think anything of it if I said I was going to spend the night at your place.'

Light dawned on Madeleine, and it was not a wholly pleasing light. 'You mean you want me to be an alibi for you, to help you to deceive Aggie? I'm to say that you're staying with me, while in fact you're off in some hotel with Terry?'

Laura avoided her aunt's eyes as she spoke. 'I was meaning even more than that. I was meaning that I actually should be in your house.'

'With Terry?'

Laura nodded, her eyes still downcast.

Madeleine let the silence linger. Her first reaction to Laura's suggestion was affront, annoyance that her niece had fixed up this meeting with such a cold-bloodedly practical intention. It had not been a sign of any *rapprochement* between the two; Laura had merely wanted something and hoped to use her aunt to get it.

155

But, as the pique receded, Madeleine saw other possibilities in the situation. First, there was the appeal of intrigue. Her role in the proceedings (which she still saw as that of Friar Laurence rather than Pandarus) was capable of considerable histrionic development, and she relished playing the scenes to which it might lead.

Also the situation offered her power over Laura, so dependent now on her aunt's decision.

'Laura,' she said, ending the silence unhelpfully as they rose to collect their earthenware mugs of decaffeinated coffee, 'I will think about it.'

And in the evening, as she lay back in her bath and did think about it, Madeleine felt good. She had got Laura back. Laura needed her. Even though what Laura needed her for was something purely practical, perhaps sordid, the dependence had been re-established.

And Madeleine also had Bernard. Bernard, who moved her so strangely and whom she seemed to have known all her life.

Her muscles relaxed. The warm water

melted away the familiar ache in her back, the bloated feeling of the day receded, and her body began again its comforting cycle of blood, as it had, regularly and without interruption, some three hundred times before in her adult life.

That same evening, Paul Grigson was alone in the house. He hadn't been to the hospital, but he had phoned the ward-sister and received the information that his mother was sleeping, but fine, there was nothing to worry about.

Paul felt his freedom trickling away. He had had the house to himself and not taken advantage of it. He shouldn't have behaved so badly with Sharon Wilkinson last time. She wasn't Madeleine and never would be, but he was further advanced with her than with any other girl, and he had to lose his virginity somehow, with someone. Maybe if he had invited her round for the evening, with no one else there. . . .

The idea brought him an instant erection. He went up to his bedroom and, lifting the top of his divan, fumbled through the folded blankets for the stock of books he kept there. If he was going to do it again, at least he'd build up a decent fantasy.

While he was looking through the books for a suitable body on which to graft Sharon's face, the doorbell rang.

Guiltily, he dropped the divan lid and went on to the landing. Then, struck by doubt, he returned to his bedroom to check that he really had put the books out of sight. He had.

When he opened the front door, he was confronted by Tony Ashton, slouched against the frame, holding a video-box in his hand.

'What do you want? Why are you here?'

Tony grinned. 'Bob said your mother was away for a day or two. Got another hot video here. Thought you might fancy seeing it.'

'No, thank you.' Paul moved to close the door, but Tony's foot prevented him.

'Why, you got someone in there?'

'No.'

'Shagging that Sharon Wilkinson, are you?'

'No, I'm not.'

Tony's grin grew broader. 'No, you're not, are you?'

'What do you mean?'

'I took her out Tuesday.'

'So? I don't care.'

'No. No, you don't, do you?'

Paul made another attempt to close the door, but Tony's foot remained fixed.

'Telling me all about you, she was. Not that there's much to tell, is there?' Tony Ashton laughed harshly. 'Ever thought of joining Virgins Anonymous, Grigson?'

This time Paul pulled the door back to swing it, and Tony prudently withdrew his foot before the slam.

But the letter-box clacked open and Paul could not shut out the voice that followed him along the hall. 'You should have had that Sharon Wilkinson. Blew your chance, you did. Take my word for it, Grigson, you missed out on quite a tasty little fuck there.'

Paul crumpled, trembling, at the foot of the stairs.

11

Since meeting Bernard, Madeleine had decided that she was going to sacrifice her long-preserved virginity. Or it might be more accurate to say that Madeleine had decided to sacrifice her long-preserved virginity and then met Bernard. He had arrived at the right time in her life and, since he passed almost all of the tests by which Madeleine judged men, she had therefore decided that he was to be the recipient of her largesse.

The tests that she applied to potential lovers were mostly social and intellectual. Looks came into it, and Bernard's height, thin frame and pained brown eyes easily qualified him there. The main physical quality that Madeleine required in a man was that he should look 'sensitive'. On that scale he scored highly.

Socially, the most important component

of a suitable man was his voice, and here again Bernard passed the test. Madeleine's antennae were delicately tuned to catch the slightest nuance of 'commonness' in any area of human behaviour, but especially in the voice. The voice was one of the first things she noticed about people. Keith's was a constant reminder of the gulf between Aggie and her latest husband. It was in part their voices that endeared Julian Garrett to Madeleine and made her feel pity for Paul Grigson.

But Bernard Hopkins had no problem with this stringent oral examination. Public school and Cambridge might have provided the polish required, though his deep, soft speech sounded so natural that it probably derived from being brought up by the right sort of parents. (Madeleine, as yet, knew little of his early background. Their conversation, when it dwelt on the past at all, tended to centre on the poignantly doomed relationship between Madeleine Severn and John Kaczmarek.)

Intellectually, too, Bernard passed with flying colours. His Upper Second in English from Cambridge seemed perfectly to complement Madeleine's Oxford Third in the same subject (won, let it be said, in the face of terrible emotional upheaval after John's death). But Bernard did not only have paper qualifications. He was still prepared—indeed happy—to sit for hours talking literature, discussing poems, listening to Madeleine reading them over a cup of coffee, for all the world as if the years had not passed and their student days were continuing on a permanent lease.

This was very comforting to Madeleine, who had found that, though her acquaintance in Brighton was varied and artistic, she had met few people who seemed to be on her intellectual level. Many were simply unwilling to talk about literature, and those who did had an irritating tendency to introduce into the conversation irrelevancies like contemporary authors or comparisons with other media. It was a huge intellectual relief to encounter a mind like Bernard's, which shared her own views and priorities on the subject of literature, and was prepared to listen to them at length.

The one detail she knew about Bernard's life which might have put off other women—the fact that he was married—seemed to Madeleine, upon consideration, a bonus rather than a disadvantage. For a start, it gave their love a tragic dimension. The mingling of Pain and Pleasure, which she so emphasised in her teaching, was immediately present. However much joy Madeleine and Bernard might derive from the relationship, at the back of their minds must always be the awareness of the potential hurt it was inflicting on his poor, crippled wife. The presence of Shirley's distant shadow also set boundaries round Madeleine and Bernard's life together. She had lived alone for a long time and, with one of those intuitive flashes of self-knowledge that occasionally came to her, recognised that she might have difficulty in adjusting to the presence of a man who could be around all the time. Most important, the fact of Bernard's marriage implied experience, which, together with his gentleness of manner, suggested he would be the ideal instrument of Madeleine's sexual initiation.

The existence of the unknown Shirley also gave the relationship, for Madeleine, a *frisson* of excitement. She liked to feel that she lived a life of mystery, that she had secrets, that there was more to Madeleine Severn than met the eye. But why, given her long history of abstinence—or at least of non-consummation—had Madeleine decided that this 'marriage of true minds' should take on a physical dimension? There had been plenty of men who had attracted her before; and plenty more who had tried their luck at seducing her, encountering initially polite, but finally intransigent, refusal. Why had Bernard been selected as the one to be favoured with Madeleine's rich gift?

The main reason was simply chronological. Madeleine had nursed and stored many of her fantasies so long that, when she examined them, even her indulgent eye could not help noticing that they were full of holes, as if some moth of the imagination had invaded their privacy and feasted on them. The greatest fantasy, of the doomed love affair with John Kaczmarek, had suffered most, and now, when she held that one up to the light, it was almost transparent and she could hardly decipher the outlines of its pattern. Though that great love was still precious, and still probably the most important event of her life, she could no longer claim to receive much support from it.

Other fantasies also looked a little threadbare in the cold light of day. The image of Madeleine Severn the *femme fatale*, the mysterious and unattainable woman for whom men lost their reason and committed acts of international folly, now did not even convince its creator. The fact that she could light a spark in Bernard should be particularly valued in the context of few other fires even smouldering.

She had also come, slowly, to acknowledge the power of sex. Probably in this process of recognition the most important factor had been the change in Laura. The estrangement of her niece had at first puzzled Madeleine. For a time she had dismissed the idea that it was a symptom of the girl's finding her own independent identity, and certainly dismissed the idea that that identity had a sexual dimension. But gradually the notion took root and grew into a suspicion, a suspicion whose reality had been confirmed at their recent lunch.

The knowledge that her niece was enjoying (albeit in the backs of cars and on golf-courses) an active sex-life had a complex effect on Madeleine. Partly she experienced a slight shock, as a mother might, but which she, in her accepted role as liberated aunt, knew that she must not express. Also, again as a mother might, she felt a growing gulf between herself and the younger woman and, with this, the need to assert her own sexual identity against the challenge of youth.

A mother whose daughter drifts away from her may feel pain, but at least she has had the experience of bearing and bringing up the child. A mother-substitute whose daughter-substitute drifts away is left empty, and Madeleine was forced to recognise her own childlessness.

This recognition ripped a large hole in the fabric of another of Madeleine's carefully folded and perfumed fantasies. She had always seen herself, not only as an extra mother to Laura, but also, in time, as a real mother. She had seen herself nursing a tiny baby, giving herself to another, imparting herself to a new individual, shaping that individual to her own outlines, regenerating a new Madeleine. In these fantasies there was very rarely a man involved, except as a distant, shadowy presence; the child was always a girl; and always, even at the moment of birth, she had red-gold hair.

While Madeleine knew she had Laura,

she had been content to nurse this fantasy, indulge it as she lay in a warm bath, cosset it as she took a solitary walk along the seafront. The fact that it was only a fantasy gave her no pain. But now Laura had demonstrated her independence, Madeleine's need to make the fantasy real was strong. And, like any woman of her age, Madeleine was aware of the pressures of time. Every month she was reminded not only of her reproductive capability, but also of the time-limit which nature had set upon it. The years were slipping away, and increasingly she needed that baby.

The coincidence of all these feelings with her meeting Bernard had made Madeleine decide to give up her virginity. But it was not a completely cold-blooded decision. She was in love with him. He stirred her in a way that no man before had done. There was a chemistry between them, a kind of chemistry which could only culminate in a physical explosion.

But it suited both to move slowly. Though Madeleine spoke always in terms of grand passions, loves at first sight and sweepings off feet, she was in reality slow to accept change. She always needed time to adjust.

Bernard, too, mindful of past failures, had no wish to rush headlong into another. He applied his own tests to Madeleine, assessing her as she had assessed him, and, though his tests were more emotional than social or intellectual, she passed, just as he had.

But, in spite of her suitability, his feelings for her troubled him. Strong emotions had always troubled him, and what he now felt was the strongest that had hit him for many years. He had contained his life, as most people do, within walls of compromise, evasions and half-truths, and, though he could recognise that the way he lived was incomplete, at least he had achieved something with which he could cope.

What he felt for Madeleine threatened that circumscribed equanimity. Part of him said: Hold back, it's never going to work, don't take the risk, it'll end in tears. But another part said: This is the great chance of your life. After all the loves that have been frustrated, you are now being offered Madeleine, and the offer will not come round again. Throw caution to the winds, have a little confidence, and retrieve some happiness from what remains of your life.

Increasingly, he knew that he had to follow the second voice.

If Madeleine and he went slowly, if they could find somewhere private, somewhere where they could be away from the strident pressures of everyday life, everything would be all right.

Those were Bernard Hopkins' thoughts as, on the Friday evening, he walked round for another 'light supper' with Madeleine Severn.

Paul Grigson's Friday had been utterly miserable. In the morning he had had a call from the hospital to say that his mother was fine, but the results of some of the tests had taken longer than expected and so the doctor wanted her to stay in over the weekend. She would be phoning her son later, and he was welcome to visit her if he wished to.

This news gave Paul only a temporary pang of anxiety. He was too preoccupied with his own troubles to have any surplus capacity for worry about anyone else.

In fact, it wasn't really a case of 'troubles' in the plural. One single trouble dominated his thoughts—the shame of his virginity. Tony Ashton's appearance the night before had devastated him. His shame seemed now to have been made public, broadcast from the rooftops, so that there could be no one left in the world who was unaware of it. Tony would have been bound to tell Bob and Sam and, once it got to them, the news would spread like wildfire. Paul felt ashamed to leave the house, afraid of people in the street pointing at him and sniggering. When the time came for him to go to the hospital for afternoon visiting, he funked it, and was rewarded by an aggrieved, recriminating phone-call from his mother.

He had always hoped that his recalcitrant virginity could be lost unobtrusively, to a prostitute perhaps, to some nameless drunken girl after a party, and the time-scale subsequently blurred, so that when the topic arose he could speak of his first time as an event from the distant past. But Tony Ashton had ruined that idea.

The shame was compounded by the other fact which Paul tried to evade, but which constantly rose up to haunt him. Not only had he not made it with Sharon Wilkinson, but Tony Ashton had. There had been no ambiguity in the older boy's statement. What pained Paul so much was not that he had been aced out, but that Tony had obviously found it so easy. All the time Paul had been going out with Sharon and being so respectful and shy, she had been panting for it. All his good manners and consideration had got Paul precisely nowhere, while Tony had just moved in for one date, no doubt stated exactly what he wanted, and got it. This knowledge made Paul feel utterly abject, as if Sharon had joined in the world's conspiracy to laugh at him.

He slumped around the house all day, his thoughts darkening into bitterness. The only image that gave him even a glimmer of comfort was that of Madeleine. *She* would understand. She knew the sort of pains he went through. He longed for her again to hold his hand as she had at their last tutorial, and to tell him that everything was going to be all right.

As it grew dark, Paul realised that he hadn't eaten since the previous evening, but he felt jumpy and nauseous and the idea of food appalled him. He went up to his bedroom, drawn by the books in his divan, but as he made to lift the lid, he realised that they would just press home his inadequacy. Only a man who can't do the real thing needs pornography.

Instead, he went to one of his drawers and took out the black-handled sheath-knife. He attached it to his belt and, facing his mirror, again drew it and went through a sequence of attacking movements.

For the first time in the day, a small feeling of power returned to him.

'We won't be the first couple to have found love and then had to keep it a secret,' said Madeleine, her voice thrillingly low.

'No,' Bernard agreed. 'The trouble is . . . it feels so good, but at this stage it also feels so fragile. We just need some time on our own, time to get to know each other, without the world coming rushing in with its hobnail boots.'

'We need somewhere magical, somewhere private, that's just for us.'

'Where do we find that, though?'

' "The grave's a fine and private place," ' Madeleine quoted wryly.

' "But none I think do there embrace," ' Bernard completed.

'So that wouldn't do for us.' Madeleine reached across to take his hand. She liked his hands. They were long-fingered, supple and strong, the sort that she identified approvingly as 'artistic'.

He returned the squeeze. 'There always seem to be people around, watching one, assessing, judging. It's difficult to feel uninhibited.'

Madeleine nodded.

He broke loose from her with unexpected suddenness, rose and paced the room fiercely. 'I'm sorry. I'm probably not going about this the right way. What do men normally do when they meet someone for whom they feel an unbearable attraction? I suppose they just ask, "Your place or mine?" and that's it. I'm sorry I'm making such a meal of it.'

This spurt of emotion took Madeleine by surprise. Till that moment, though she had never doubted the depth of Bernard's feelings, they had always been expressed quietly, as if through sadness. His sudden energy shocked and rather excited her.

She went across to him and laid her hands on his shoulders. His eyes, as if ashamed of having given away so much of himself, avoided hers.

'I think you're going about it in just the right way,' Madeleine said softly. 'I'm not the kind of woman,' she continued with some hauteur, 'who goes for the "Your place or mine?" approach. You recognise the seriousness of what has happened to us, and I respect you for that.'

'Thank you.' Still he did not look at her.

'Anyway,' she went on, in a lighter voice, ' "Your place or mine?" doesn't really fit our circumstances, does it? We can hardly go to your place.'

'No,' he agreed. 'There are too many memories there.'

'Not to mention your wife.'

He nodded slowly as he repeated, 'Not to mention my wife.'

'And here we are in my place, and somehow that too . . . is not right.'

She did not know exactly why she said this, but she felt it strongly. Her own neat little house did not seem a suitable setting for the great sacrifice of her virginity. She wanted to start the new phase of her life on neutral ground. She loved Bernard, she welcomed him for 'light suppers' with the curfew of his appointments at the Metropole Hotel, but she did not want him there all the time. And she had an imprecise but strong feeling that letting him share her little bed upstairs would confer some kind of territorial rights.

He did not question what she said, apparently agreeing with the ground-rules she had drawn up. There was a long silence, during which he seemed more than once on the verge of speaking, but each time he withdrew. When words finally did come, they were thick with strain.

'Madeleine, would you . . . Please say no if that's what you mean. I won't be offended. Madeleine, would you. . . .' After the hesitations, he spoke the last sentence in a burst. 'If I were to rent somewhere, somewhere quiet, private, would you come away for a weekend with me?'

Tension gleamed in his eyes. Madeleine could sense how much he depended on her reply. She smiled and, bountifully, said, 'Yes, Bernard. Yes, I would.'

Their kiss in the hall was not long, but it expressed a deep complicity. The agreement had been made. Now only the details remained to be arranged.

Bernard walked briskly away from Madeleine's door without a backward glance, so he did not see the figure concealed behind a tree on the other side of the road.

Paul Grigson recognised the back view of his rival and fingered the black handle of his sheath-knife. For a moment he contemplated following Bernard, but he hadn't the energy. After the clashing emotions of the day, he now felt exhausted. Apathy washed over him.

He was not even very clear as to why he was there, what he had wanted to say to Madeleine, what he had hoped for in return. He had just been aware of the dominating urge to rush down to Kemp Town.

And now he was there, the wave of compulsion had broken. He felt a little stupid and very, very tired.

Wearily, he started to walk back home again.

12

Bernard Hopkins was a meticulous planner. He knew himself well enough to realise that loose ends in any arrangements upset him, and so he always made elaborate preparations, checking and rechecking every detail until he felt confident that nothing could go wrong.

His mother, though now dead for five years, had always been a strong influence on him and he recalled that once, when she had been booking a holiday just after his father's death, she had consulted the small ads in that organ of gentility, the *Lady*, asserting that that was where 'the nicer sort of property' was likely to be advertised.

On the Saturday morning therefore he went out and bought a copy of the *Lady* and, with that and the telephone on the table beside him, he consulted the large-scale AA road map which had belonged to his father.

He knew enough of Madeleine to be certain that she would not wish to be involved in the arrangements. She would not want to go through the minutiae of choosing an area, finding suitable accommodation and fixing the rental. In her fastidious mind, the word 'detail' was almost invariably accompanied by the epithet 'sordid'. What she would like from Bernard would be a *fait accompli,* to be presented suddenly with the address of the romantic venue where their love could be allowed to blossom. Bernard was determined that that was how it should be.

The first priority was to choose an area. Common sense told him that neither of them would wish to travel far and that therefore the property should be an hour's—or at most an hour and a half's—drive from Brighton. There were plenty of remote parts of Sussex and Hampshire where, he felt sure, suitable cottages must exist.

From the start he had known that the place should be a country cottage, though he could not precisely define why. Partly, it was a kind of generalised sentimentality, the influence of English Tourist Board brochures, the illusion of peace that thatch and beams invariably prompt. As well, although he did not realise it, he was being called back to his youth, times when his father had been working and he had holidayed alone with his mother, times of peace before adolescence had shaken into fragments the simple pattern of his childhood.

Having drawn a mental radius from Brighton to establish his area of search, he turned to the classified advertisement section of the *Lady,* where he found a profusion of country cottages available for rental. Most of the details specified the location of the property, so he was able within a short time to compile a list of some half-dozen which sounded to be possibilities.

He began to telephone the owners.

There was no question of his making the booking in the name of Bernard Hopkins. Caution—even deviousness—came naturally to him, and he had caught some of Madeleine's excitement at the prospect of a clandestine liaison. Besides, there were people who must remain ignorant of his plans; he had to cover his tracks.

Identifying himself as Mr Edward Farrar, Bernard enquired courteously of each owner whether their advertised property might be free for rental for the weekend after next, the 2nd to 4th November (this being the date which Madeleine and he had agreed as suitable for their great adventure).

To those owners whose properties were free, Bernard addressed a series of detailed questions about the location, appearance and amenities of their cottages. He made notes of the answers he received, and referred frequently to his map. He closed each conversation politely, having checked methods of payment for the rental, and in two cases said that he would hope to ring again when he had sorted out his own plans.

The two addresses which remained on his short-list were Sea Spray Cottage, near Sidlesham, just to the west of Bognor Regis, and Winter Jasmine Cottage, near Shorton, some four miles north-east of Pulborough. Both, according to their owners, were remote, the first set on a spit of land into the sea off a shingle beach, the second at the end of a three-mile drive which had once led to some now-demolished farm buildings. The owner of Sea Spray Cottage had a Bognor Regis telephone number, the owner of Winter Jasmine Cottage a London one.

The first was a man, with a voice of deterrent heartiness; the second sounded to be an old lady, slightly vague, slightly flustered by the enquiry.

This last fact put Bernard in favour of Winter Jasmine Cottage. The old lady seemed more likely to swallow the false name and other necessary duplicities. But Bernard was a methodical man. He was not going to make a hasty decision. The real test of the two properties would be what they looked like. He was determined to present Madeleine with an appropriately romantic setting.

He got into his five-year-old brown Austin Maxi and set off on a tour of inspection.

As he drove, Bernard's mind was full of images of Madeleine. These images were sexual, but imprecise, like shots through a vaselined lens in a television commercial. There was Madeleine warm in bed, in a flowing white robe, a Madeleine who looked up at him in gratitude and understanding as he crossed to open the curtains and let the morning light in on the scene of their love. Through tiny leaded windows he saw, alternately, the sparkling splendour of the sea, and then sweeps of downland, brown and russet, half-stripped trees touched by autumn sun. It would all depend on which was the right cottage.

As soon as he saw it, he knew that Sea Spray Cottage was wrong. Its drab, unpainted pebble-dash made the walls look flimsy, as if constructed of egg-boxes. The blue paint on the salt-eroded window-frames was faded and sad. Sea Spray Cottage had about it an air of melancholy, but of bleak rather than romantic melancholy. It was not right.

It took him a little while to find the turning off to Winter Jasmine Cottage. There was a small white sign at the head of the farm track, but its post leant back into nettles and the surface was mottled with green. However, on his third slow drive past, he saw it and was able to decipher the overgrown lettering. He turned the car off down the track.

The surface was scarred and pitted by tractor-wheels, but the growth of grass over the ridges suggested that none had passed that way for some years. Bernard drove with care, worried for the safety of his car's exhaust-pipe. Twice he had to get out to open gates. On marks for remoteness, Winter Jasmine Cottage scored highly.

He turned the corner of a shaggy grove of trees, and saw it.

The thatch came down low, so low that only a child could have stood upright beneath its eaves. Tiny windows in the white-washed frontage flanked a red-painted door. Set into the thatch above this was a kind of dormer, a small leaded window, presumably from the bedroom.

The garden was an autumn wilderness, to which the sunlight imparted a spurious glow of colour. An untidy laurel hedge fronted it and grew higher and more wild round the vehicle entrance at the side.

Bernard breathed deeply. Winter Jasmine Cottage was ideal.

He rang the old lady with the London number as soon as he got back. Yes, he would like the cottage for the weekend he had mentioned.

Oh good, the old lady was delighted. It wasn't easy living on a pension these days and every let helped. Then, with great diffidence, she apologised that, 'due to unhappy experiences in the past', she now had to insist on a deposit being paid. She didn't like to sound mercenary, but so many people these days, even the nicest-seeming people, turned out not to be what they appeared that—

Don't worry, Mr Farrar assured her, he had fully expected to pay a deposit. In fact, why didn't he send her the full amount of the rental straight away, in cash? Then the sordid business side would all be dealt with, and she could send him the key.

Oh well, that was kind. It would certainly be a great weight off her mind to have that sorted out. Now, the key. . . . Yes, she could send him one. . . . Or sometimes she arranged that Mrs Rankin, the lady who came in to clean the cottage, was there to let the tenants in. . . . They even sometimes— and she knew this was rather naughty, but she was a good judge of people and she could tell just from his voice that Mr Farrar was an honest sort of man—left the key under the water-butt round the back.

The last method would be fine, said Mr Farrar. Just fine. No need to trouble Mrs Rankin, just leave the key under the water-butt.

Mrs Waterstone (which was the old lady's name) then said that she would send Mr

Farrar the details about the cottage, map, terms of rental and so on. Where should she send them to?

He had prepared for this. Close by his own house was one that was empty. The owners had gone away for six months and left him a key 'in case of emergency'. He gave that address and confirmed that his name was Mr Edward Farrar.

'Oh,' said Mrs Waterstone as a final thought, 'I'm afraid that, though blankets are provided, tenants are expected to bring their own sheets.'

'That'll be fine, Mrs Waterstone,' said Mr Edward Farrar.

As soon as he had put the phone down, Bernard Hopkins reached for his wallet and counted out some of the notes he had drawn from his Post Office Savings Account for the purpose, placed them in an envelope, added a charming covering letter headed with his absent neighbours' address, and took the package to the post-box on the corner.

He felt satisfied with his day's work. A few more details must be sorted out and then all would be ready for him and Madeleine.

Sharon Wilkinson had been surprised when Tony Ashton rang again and asked her out on the Saturday night. She had expected, after their acrimonious parting earlier in the week, that she would hear no more from him.

At first she thought she should go all frosty and refuse the invitation, but when it came to it, she couldn't see any good reason to do so. She was an equable soul who didn't bear grudges. Besides, Tony had asked her out to a disco and she longed to see if he was as good a dancer as her friend at Boots claimed.

There was also the other factor—which she tried to deny but couldn't—that she was very attracted to him. But if he tried any more of that funny stuff, he wasn't going to get anywhere. She had had time to sort out her reactions since the embarrassment of their earlier encounter, and she reckoned she now had more control of herself. Tony Ashton had not got a job, he wore an earring, and was therefore not Mr Right. He might be fun to be with, fun to dance with, fun to kiss even, but there was no way that he was going to make any withdrawals from the account that she was saving for marriage.

He was also in for a shock if he tried the same sort of thing on the Saturday evening. Sharon's father would not be in the pub; he was laid up with 'flu and would be in bed directly above the sitting-room where the previous advances had been made. But Sharon didn't mention that to Tony at the beginning of their date. She didn't want to spoil a nice, safe evening's dancing.

So she was quite happy for him to put his arm round her shoulders and give her the odd kiss as they walked along from her house to the bus-stop. Sharon felt once more in control. She was pleased to be with someone who attracted her, secure in the knowledge that her virginity was not at risk.

Had Tony known what she was thinking, he might have proved a less attentive escort.

And had Paul Grigson, who saw them walking past together out of his bedroom window, known the true state of their relationship, the pain which seared across his mind might have been less acute.

13

It had to be the same disguise. The clothes and glasses had become part of a ritual, props for his other identity. Once he had made the decision about what he had to do, he packed the clothes quickly into his old school-bag and left the empty house. Again the change of personality had to happen at Brighton Station. A pattern had been established.

Early on a Saturday evening there were inevitably more comings and goings to the gents than on his previous mid-morning visit, but no one looked twice at the tall figure with a bag who put his coin into the slot and entered one of the cubicles. Inside, he changed slowly, with meticulous care, into the brown herring-bone jacket and the dark grey flannel trousers. He donned the duffel coat, again poignantly aware of the tobacco smell of his father.

Finally, he put on the glasses and once again, as the world blurred around him, felt reassuringly invisible, as if he had erased his own personality completely.

He waited for a full five minutes, sitting on the lavatory seat, breathing deeply and evenly. Then he picked up the bag, left the cubicle, went into the station, bought a ticket, and caught the next train to Victoria. Again, no one gave him a second glance.

Because it was Saturday night, Soho was busy, full of rowdy drunks and tourists in search of prurient entertainment. This time he did not go into the crowded sex-shops or join the queues for a quick flash in the peep shows. The lust in him was urgent enough without such titillation.

Just as the disguise had had to be the same, so it had to be the same prostitute. The unseen 'Mandy' had joined the repertory company of his fantasies and it was unthinkable that he should go to anyone else.

The alley off Wardour Street was crowded with sauntering couples having a night 'up West', youths spilling out of the topless bar, a few men loitering purposefully against the railings, potential customers perhaps for

'Mandy' or 'Cleo'.

He ignored everyone around him and walked in through the doorway, up the bare boards of the stairs, and onto the landing. Without pausing to think, he banged on the grey fireproofed door. Again, so quickly that he wondered whether there was some hidden warning-bell downstairs, the latch unclicked, the door opened a crack, and the maid's shrivelled face showed.

He said nothing.

'The young lady's busy at the moment. Could you come back in ten minutes.'

'I'll wait.'

The maid shrugged and the door snapped closed again.

He was calm now. The pounding of his heart had settled down. It would be all right this time. Finally, the burden would be shed. His penis was painfully rigid. Another quarter of an hour and the great hurdle would be surmounted.

Footsteps boomed on the stairs. He turned and, through the blur of his lenses, saw a figure in a bright blue nylon anorak approaching the landing. The figure took him in at the same moment, swayed uncertainly, then vanished back into the darkness. Coward. He felt a kind of superiority at the strength of his own resolution.

There was another click from the grey door, a rattle of the chain and it opened. A man in a dark overcoat with its collar turned up sidled out and, with head averted, scuttled off down the stairs.

The maid's wizened face looked out and took in his presence. She beckoned with her head. He followed her in.

The first small box, the maid's room, contained a couple of ragged easy-chairs, a low table and a mobile Calor Gas heater. On one wall a gratuitous mantelpiece had been stuck (though there was no fireplace), and on top of it was a bowl with a dusty display of plastic flowers. The thin cord carpet was discoloured and lay on the uneven floorboards without underlay. From behind the interior door came the sound of water running into a sink.

'Young lady won't be a moment,' said the maid. 'Care to sit down?'

He subsided into one of the chairs; the springs dug into his buttocks. Still, he felt calm. Still, he felt randy.

The water in the next room stopped running, and the door behind him opened. He half-turned to see a sulky girl with frizzed-out black hair. Her skin was white, but the set of her features suggested West Indian ancestry. She had a shiny cream house-coat wrapped around her.

Her eyes took no notice of him, but went straight to the maid. 'I'm out of cigarettes. Could you get some?'

The maid looked doubtful. 'Are you sure?'

For the first time, 'Mandy' looked at him. A glance seemed sufficient to convince her. With an edge of contempt, she said, 'Yes.'

Still looking doubtful, the maid reached for a handbag and moved arthritically to the exterior door.

'Mandy' flicked her head towards the bedroom, and he followed her in. She arranged herself on the bed in a pose of uninterested coquetry. 'Right, what do you want?'

Her voice had a flat, Midland flavour.

'Well, sex,' he replied thickly.

She let out a harsh, unamused laugh. 'I guessed that. This isn't a chip-shop. But there are different sorts of sex and they cost differently. There's straight or there's—'

'Straight,' he interrupted.

She named the price. The money from the Post Office Savings Account would cover it. He drew out the notes. She nodded towards the bedside-table and he put the money there.

She tugged the belt of her housecoat loose and splayed her legs on the bed. He caught a glimpse of dark hair, and averted his eyes as he slipped off his father's duffel-coat and reached to undo his tie.

'Not the lot,' came the girl's voice harshly. 'Just the trousers. You're not here for the night.'

He released the belt of his trousers and they dropped to the floor. But as he lowered his underpants, he knew it had gone wrong. The stiff flesh, desperate for relief, had melted in an instant to nothing. He froze, trying to summon to his mind some image that would make him a man again.

'Come on,' said the girl's voice. 'We haven't got all night.' She was not sufficiently interested to notice his depleted state.

He moved towards her. Maybe physical contact would bring it back. Maybe he needed the stimulus of her flesh. He laid himself tentatively on top of her.

At once, her bored but practised hands

were reaching out for him, reaching to feed him into her, reaching for the nothing that hung between his legs.

Her face was very close to his. He could smell a hint of garlic on her breath. He could see her lip curl as she said, 'Not going to get far with *that*, are we?'

Before he knew it, his hands had closed on her throat. Her eyes widened in horror. Her hands moved to fend him off, but suddenly he was strong and he pinioned her arms with his elbows.

Her body twitched in desperation. Her legs thrashed, trying to force him off. A choking cry started from her lips, but he tightened the ring of his long fingers and the cry died in breathy gurgling.

He felt a sense of power. He had the strength. He could do it.

The twitching subsided. Her movements slowed. The eyes, formerly popping out with fear, now rolled. Her lips parted and the tongue protruded. A little froth gathered at the corners of her mouth. Hazily, through the glasses, he watched her body grow still.

He kept the grip around her throat for another minute, then slowly released it, and there was no more challenge, no more mockery.

He straightened up till he was kneeling over her, and became aware of the fiercely rigid flesh of his penis. He hardly had to touch it before the jet of semen spurted, leaving a broken snail-track across her house-coat-clad shoulder, her cheek, the black frizzed hair.

He pulled up his underpants and trousers, rezipped, and replaced his father's duffel-coat. The glasses had stayed on throughout the three minutes of his stay.

He glanced quickly round the room. Some instinct for security made him take back his money, fearing fingerprints.

He opened the door and moved quickly, but not hurriedly, down the stairs. He darted out into the alley, turning left, and was lost in the crowd before the maid with dyed red hair had reached the doorway with her redundant supplies of cigarettes.

He kept the glasses on on the train back to Brighton. Still they seemed to insulate him, keep him apart from what had happened.

He managed almost completely to block it out of his mind. It had been so quick, he could almost convince himself that it had been a dream, another episode in the strange tangle of fantasy that at times seemed to take him over.

All he felt was the rueful sense of another failure. He had got it wrong. His approach had been wrong. Indulgently, he ticked himself off for lack of self-knowledge.

Why on earth should he have imagined it would work with a nameless whore? He was too sensitive for that. What he needed was someone gentle, someone loving, who would not rush him, who would understand his inexperience.

It would be different, he knew, with Madeleine.

14

Paul now carried the black-handled sheath-knife with him wherever he went. He felt challenged in every aspect of his life, and the knife gave him a kind of security.

His mind was more tangled than ever. There seemed to be so many new things to worry about that the space inside was crammed to bursting. There was the public shame of what Tony Ashton and Sharon were doing, and of what they must be saying about him. In the background was a dark cloud of anxiety about his mother, whom the hospital still wished to keep in for observation. And other, darker images fought their way through from time to time to the surface of his fears.

Increasingly, the only thought which gave him any peace was that of Madeleine. He kept reliving the moment when she had held his hand, when he had been so close to her, and it seemed that that was the only occasion in the past weeks when he had felt complete, when he had felt human, not swamped with threats from everything he saw around him. He ached for the moment of their next tutorial. In her presence he felt sure he would once again be whole, healed at least for the duration of their proximity.

It was Shelley this time. Paul had battled for some days against his vagrant concentration to read some of the poet's work, but he had found it hard going. Most of the lines blurred as he read them, sense slipping by in a cascade of words, and the bits he could understand he didn't much care for. With Keats, though he had found the language difficult, he had at least got some feeling of the opulence of the poet's imagination. Byron, though again obscured by archaic usage, did retain a kind of romantic appeal, arising more from what he had found out of the poet's life-style than from his writings. 'Childe Harold' in particular, when Paul thought about it, offered grim parallels for his own alienation. But Shelley. . . . It all just seemed to be words. There was passion there, obviously, but not a kind of passion which he could identify with any of the many he had experienced himself.

It was clear from the start that Madeleine did not share his view. 'But, Paul, can't you *see?* Shelley is the most modern of poets. I mean, I would have thought, of all the Romantics, he has most to say to young people today.'

'He doesn't say a lot to me,' Paul ventured a grin as he made this admission. He felt at peace, relaxed. He was with Madeleine, her perfume surrounded him. There were a lot of things still to be sorted out, but it would all be all right in the end. She would be his and his life would be transformed by her love.

'Oh, come *on*. Shelley talks the language of idealism, of peace and love.'

'I don't understand what you mean.'

'Well, those are the values of the young, aren't they? They always have been.'

Paul projected his lower lip dubiously. 'I'm not sure. I don't think many people I know are very idealistic. Most of them are just out for what they can get.' The image of Tony Ashton and Sharon flashed uncomfortably across his mind.

'But no, Paul, the young *are* idealists. They must be. For example, I'm sure all of your friends are anti-war.'

'Wouldn't say so. Most of them got really excited when the Falklands thing was on. Couldn't wait to get out there and bash a few Argies.'

'Well, maybe, but nuclear war . . . I mean most of them must want the bomb banned.'

Again he didn't seem convinced. 'No, I think most of them reckon there's not a lot you can do about it. It's going to happen. We're all going to be blown to blazes in a few years, so you may as well get what you can out of life while you're still around.'

Madeleine began to feel that maybe she wasn't getting her message across. 'But what about Human Rights? I mean democracy. You mentioned the Falklands. Well, I didn't actually approve of what went on then, but it could be seen as a blow for freedom against a repressive regime. Exactly the sort of thing Shelley was recommending in his 'Ode to Liberty'. I mean, when he writes. . . .' She dropped into her recitation voice.

*'Oh, that the free would stamp the
impious name
Of KING into the dust! or write it
there,
So that this blot upon the page of fame
Were as a serpent's path, which the
light air
Erases, and the flat sands close behind!'*

She paused impressively, but Paul still didn't look impressed, so she changed tack. 'What about Shelley's atheism then? Surely that's something that strikes a chord with your generation?'

'Not really,' said Paul. 'Not particularly. I mean, nobody I know believes in God anyway, so it's not really a very big deal.' He did not feel that he was being rude to Madeleine; he thought he was showing his character, fencing with her as an intellectual equal.

'His belief in Free Love then? Now that really did put him ahead of his time. He had all the ideas of Open Marriage and what-have-you long before they were fashionable. Love was the dominant force for him. You get it stated in 'Prometheus Unbound'. He writes "and yet I feel most vain

201

all hopes but love." Surely that must have some appeal to the young. I mean, the young are the love generation.'

Paul looked at her in puzzlement, and even to Madeleine came an inkling that what she was saying might perhaps be out of date, that she was transferring her own youth on to his. 'Well, maybe not,' she conceded briskly, retreating.

'I don't think many of the people I know of my age are that hooked on love,' Paul began slowly. Then, summoning courage, he said, '*I* think love's very important. It's important to me. In fact, it's probably *the* most important thing in the world for me.'

Madeleine smiled, unaware of the direction in which his remarks were leading. It was nice, she thought, to hear such a charming sentiment from him. His reactions to Shelley had sounded a bit negative and it was encouraging to know that he didn't really share the depressing nihilism which seemed to have taken over young people in the years since she had been one of them.

'What I really mean,' Paul picked his way gingerly onwards, 'is that being with someone I love is the only thing that keeps me going. I really think I'd crack up if I didn't go on seeing the person I love.'

He hesitated, and, as had happened once before, his declaration was averted by the door's opening.

This time it was not Bernard who came in, but Julian Garrett's secretary, Stella Franklin.

'Oh, Madeleine, sorry to interrupt.' She condescended a little smile to Paul and held out a letter. 'It's just that I wasn't sure whether or not you'd be dropping into the office this morning and this was left for you. Didn't want you to miss it.'

Madeleine took the envelope and said in a politely dismissive tone, 'Oh, thank you, Stella.'

But Mrs Franklin lingered. 'It's from Bernard. He was hoping to hand it over, but Julian had to send him out to a group of Italians who were booked into one of the other schools and had their class cancelled.'

'Ah.' Madeleine managed to put the minimum of interest into the monosyllable, but still it didn't seem enough to dismiss Mrs Franklin.

'Always happy to be the messenger,' the older woman said, with a hint of coquetry which didn't suit her.

'It's a booklist on Tennyson that Bernard promised to look out for me,' said Madeleine frostily.

This had the desired effect. It even made Mrs Franklin look slightly discomfited, which was a rare sight. She also appeared to believe what Madeleine said and her face showed the dismantling of the cosy fantasy she had been building up.

'Ah, yes. Yes, of course,' she said, and left the room.

'Now, where were we?' asked Madeleine, her concentration broken.

'We were talking about love,' said Paul. Then, losing his nerve, 'Shelley and love.'

'Oh, yes,' she said, and then repeated the word more firmly. 'Yes.' But the distraction of the letter was too great. 'Excuse me a moment,' she said, as she ran her finger along the inside of the envelope.

She half-pulled the contents out, then, seeing their nature, pushed them back into the envelope, which she shoved into her handbag, quickly. But not quickly enough. Paul had had time to see the colours of a reproduction of a painting. The envelope contained a greetings card. It seemed an unlikely way of presenting a booklist.

'As I thought,' Madeleine said, with a businesslike exhalation of air. 'Now, Shelley . . . Shelley and love, that's where we were, isn't it?'

Paul couldn't answer. Depression had descended on him like a dark hood. He knew he had been fooling himself. He had entertained the pleasing fantasy of Madeleine and himself and had managed to shut out the fact of Bernard's existence. But the card had removed that illusion. Madeleine's reaction, her sudden decision not to read it left him in no doubt that it was a love-letter. Bernard Hopkins possessed Madeleine just as completely as Tony Ashton possessed Sharon. Once again Paul was the butt, aced out, a laughing stock. Thank God he hadn't got further in his declaration, hadn't made a complete fool of himself by exposing his love.

Madeleine looked at him, and his face must have reflected the shift of his mood, because she asked, 'What's the matter?'

He shook his head. He couldn't tell her the truth. 'I don't know. Everything.'

Her voice was gentle and, as he half-hoped, half-feared she might, she leant towards him. 'Is it still girl trouble, Paul?'

He gave his head a little shake and found, to his shame and despair, that he was crying. He looked away, but she had seen the tears.

'Oh, Paul, Paul, you mustn't take things so to heart.' Once again Madeleine felt strong, filled with maternal power. She could help this boy. 'What's wrong? What has Sharon done to get you like this? Has she given you the brush-off?'

'No, it's not Sharon. It's nothing to do with her.' And yet it was, partly. Sharon's going off with Tony, Sharon's going to bed with Tony, was part of the confusion. But it was more than that, it was all the diverse moods and personalities inside him, the different people he could be at different times, the impossibility of reconciling them into one person, that seemed to be destroying him.

'Then is there something wrong at home?' asked Madeleine.

That at least gave him a safe, acceptable answer. 'It's my mother,' he said brokenly, although he knew it wasn't really. 'She's in hospital. They're doing tests. She's been in for a week now.'

'You poor boy.' Once again, as he had

feared she might, Madeleine took his hand. He turned slightly away. 'She'll be all right, Paul. I'm sure she'll be all right. Do you know what the tests are for?'

He shook his head, feeling hypocritical. She was giving him sympathy for his mother's illness and it seemed to him that he hardly thought about his mother.

'You mustn't let yourself get depressed about it, Paul.'

He snorted a bitter laugh. 'Easy to say.'

'Do you get very depressed?'

Still not looking at her, not trusting himself so close, he mumbled, 'I suppose that's a good word to describe it.' But the word didn't seem adequate for the violent seesawing moods that possessed him.

'And what do you think when you're depressed?' Madeleine persisted.

'I don't know. Just that it all seems hopeless. That I don't have any future. That there's no point in going on.'

'You mustn't think that.' Madeleine's second hand came to enclose his. He turned even further away and, as he did so, his pullover rode up to show the end of the sheath-knife on his belt.

'What's that?' asked Madeleine in alarm.

He turned to look. 'That? Oh. Just a knife.'

'Why do you carry a knife?'

'I don't know.'

'You must know.'

'Well, yes, perhaps. I suppose I just carry it in case I need it.'

'Why should you need it?'

He shrugged and looked away again. Madeleine let go of his hands and sat upright in her seat. 'Give it to me, Paul.'

'What?'

'Give me the knife.'

'Why?'

'You're in a disturbed state. I don't think you should be carrying a knife. Besides,' she continued, improvising, 'it's a rule in this school that none of the students should carry offensive weapons. Come on, give it to me.'

Wordlessly, in a numb, almost hypnotic state, Paul unbuckled his belt, slipped the sheath-knife off it, and passed the weapon over to Madeleine.

'Thank you.' She rose to her feet. 'I'm afraid I'm going to have to hand this over to Mr Garrett.'

She left the room.

'Just give it back to him,' said Julian Garrett.

'I can't do that.'

'Why not? It's his.'

'But, Julian, you can't have students walking into the school with weapons like this.'

'Who can be hurt? There are hardly any other students around at the moment.'

'But it's the principle.'

'This isn't a comprehensive. The boy's eighteen. If he wants to carry a knife, and so long as he doesn't stab anyone with it, I don't see why we should bother to object.'

'I'm not so worried about him stabbing someone else. I'm worried about him doing himself an injury.'

'Why should he?'

'He's a very confused young man. Very depressed. He was virtually talking about suicide a few moments ago.'

Julian Garrett sighed, shook his head, and picked a hair off his elegantly pin-striped sleeve. 'Madeleine, I don't usually have to say this to you. Garrettway is not a full residential school. All we have to do is teach the students what they pay for. We're not responsible for their personal problems. There's no need for us to get involved.'

'Sometimes you have to get involved, Julian.'

'Not in my experience,' said her employer, with a sardonic smile.

Madeleine nodded sharply and went out of the room. The encounter had left them both feeling good. Madeleine had dramatised herself into a crusader, fighting nobly for the rights and welfare of her pupils against an unfeeling management. And Julian had got his customary satisfaction from another responsibility evaded.

He thought idly of Madeleine after she had gone. She had been looking good that morning, the flush of annoyance heightening the colour of her cheeks, throwing into relief, as ever, the red-gold hair. Julian wondered, not for the first time, why he, with his strong appetite for women, had never fancied her. Partly, he knew, it was circumstance. She was too close to him, too ever-present, and he always took care that his exit-route should be clear before starting any relationship.

But it wasn't just that.

For a full minute after Madeleine had left the room, Paul resisted the temptation, but he knew he would succumb sooner or later, and it would be safer to succumb sooner.

He reached into her handbag and extracted the envelope. He slid the card out. The picture was a reproduction of Holman Hunt's *Claudio and Isabella*, but Paul did not recognise it. He did not know that it illustrated the moment from *Measure for Measure* when Claudio tries to persuade his sister to sacrifice her virginity and save his life. Nor, to be fair, had the card's sender thought of that particular significance when he chose it. So far as Bernard Hopkins was concerned, he knew that Madeleine liked the Pre-Raphaelites and he had thought the card romantic.

The message inside, which Paul read, Bernard had also thought romantic.

MADELEINE—YOU ARE CORDIALLY INVITED TO SPEND THE WEEKEND OF 2ND TO 4TH NOVEMBER AT WINTER JASMINE COTTAGE, SHORTON, NR PULBOROUGH, WEST SUSSEX. RSVP.

Paul only opened the card long enough to

read the words before he put it back into its envelope and returned it to Madeleine's handbag.

But he had had time to memorise the address.

Madeleine did not want to give the knife back to Paul. She was mildly worried that he might do himself some injury with it, but, more than that, she didn't want the drama of her confiscation to end in bathos. So she put it in the bottom of her brief-case which hung on a hook with her coat outside the office.

15

'Oh, thank goodness it's you.'

Bernard recognised the voice at the other end as soon as he picked up the phone. 'Madeleine. Why shouldn't it be me?'

'I was afraid your wife might answer. I suppose I'd just have rung off if she had.'

'You needn't worry. I always answer the phone.'

'You're more mobile, I suppose, than she is.'

Bernard neither confirmed nor denied this. 'Just assume that you're safe to ring me.'

'And she can't hear your end of the conversation?'

'The telephone's in my study.'

Madeleine sighed with relief. 'It's amazing how quickly one slips into the usages of duplicity. Secret phone-calls, secret messages.'

'Yes.' Bernard did not appear to wish to pursue this topic. He sounded expectant, waiting for something from her.

'I rang,' said Madeleine slowly, 'in response to your invitation.'

'Yes?'

'Being a nicely brought-up lady, I know that one should reply to invitations promptly. I know it should really be done by letter, but I wasn't sure who picked up the post in your house.'

'I do that too.'

'I wasn't to know that. So, anyway, the invitation. . . .' She let the silence spread for a moment before continuing. 'Now, let me get the form of words right.' She spoke as if quoting an official document. 'Madeleine Severn has much pleasure in accepting Bernard Hopkins' kind invitation to Winter Jasmine Cottage for the weekend of the 2nd to the 4th of November.'

'Oh. Good.' Bernard could not disguise the relief in his voice. 'I'm very glad to hear that.'

'No, I'll look forward to it. Winter Jasmine Cottage—it sounds beautiful.'

'It is. I've been to have a look.'

'I have visions of a magic place, beams,

thatched roof, surrounded by the yellow blooms of winter jasmine.'

'I can do you the beams and the thatched roof all right, Madeleine. I'm afraid the winter jasmine isn't out yet. Too early for it.'

'Oh, well. Can't have everything. I'm sure it'll still be lovely.'

'Yes. I hope so,' he said gently, but with a note of seriousness.

'Thank you for making all the arrangements, Bernard. Is there anything I can do to help?'

'Well, I suppose we ought to think about food.'

'Leave that to me. I'll work out menus for the whole weekend.'

'Thank you. I'll organise some wine.'

'Anything else?'

'Oh, the owner said, um . . .' Bernard was suddenly embarrassed, 'there aren't any sheets in the cottage.'

'I'll bring some.'

'Well, I can if—'

'I'll do it.'

Bernard let out a little, nervous laugh. 'It was really quite easy. It's amazing how easily things can be done if you set your mind to it.'

'Yes.' Then, with a hint of reproof, Madeleine said, 'We must be discreet, Bernard.'

'I know.'

'I mean you shouldn't really have given that card to Stella Franklin. You know what a gossip she is.'

'Yes, I know. It was daft. It's just that I was so convinced I'd see you at the Garrettway, I had the card all ready to slip to you discreetly, and then I was suddenly sent off to deal with these Italians. And I just wanted you to have it as soon as possible. I couldn't wait. I didn't give it to Stella, anyway. I just put it in your pigeon-hole.'

'And she took it upon herself to make it a personal delivery.'

'She must have done. Do you think she suspects what's going on, Madeleine?'

'I think I managed to put her off the scent this time. But we must be careful. I couldn't bear the thought of this getting back to your wife.'

'No. No.' Bernard sounded subdued for the rest of the conversation, and after the call had ended he sat for some time in troubled contemplation. Madeleine's mention of his wife had brought home to him the reality of what he was doing, and he felt guilt for his duplicity.

Why, Madeleine wondered again as she looked at her niece over the health-food restaurant table, did Laura do her hair like that? Surely no one could imagine that the shaved nape and the flopping blonded forelock was attractive. It might be fashionable, but people ought to be able to recognise when a fashion was ugly.

Madeleine smoothed down her shaggy loam-coloured pullover, her fingers lightly caressing the stomach into which a nut rissole and yoghurt with honey had just disappeared. 'Laura,' she said, 'I've been thinking about what you asked me when we met last week.'

'Yes?' The girl's voice was tense, very dependent on the reaction, so Madeleine did not hurry too much in replying.

'I still don't like the idea of deceiving Aggie. . . .'

Laura looked downcast and petulant.

'On the other hand, as you know, I've always believed in the importance of love, and I think there are times when one must put love above other considerations.'

Laura looked up, hopeful now, but impatient.

'You are sure that you're in love with this Terry?'

'Absolutely certain. We're just right for each other. It works.'

'Good.' Another dramatic pause was allowed to go the distance, before the sudden question, 'Would you like to come and stay at my house from the 2nd to the 4th of November?'

Laura looked wary. 'You mean, with Terry?'

Madeleine nodded bountifully.

Laura leapt from her seat, threw her arms round her aunt, and kissed her. 'You're great. I knew you wouldn't let me down.'

Madeleine was warmed by the embrace. She remembered how easily and frequently Laura had used to hug her, and she felt that more of the recent distance between them had been closed.

Laura sat down, still smiling ecstatically. Then a shadow of doubt clouded her face. 'But that's a weekend, isn't it?'

'Yes. Friday night and Saturday night.'

'Terry goes back to Worcester at weekends, to see his mother.'

'Couldn't she forego seeing him for one weekend?'

'Maybe,' said Laura dubiously. 'Perhaps he could stay down the Friday night and then leave the Saturday morning. I'd have to check.'

'It's up to you to sort out the details.' There was some asperity in Madeleine's voice. She did not like having the teeth of her gift horse examined so minutely. 'I thought you wanted me to act as an alibi and that's what I'm offering to do for you. If you don't want to take up the offer, then that's up to you.'

Warned by her aunt's tone, and realising that the opportunity might establish a useful precedent, Laura was instantly conciliatory. 'I'm sorry, Madeleine. I didn't mean it like that at all. No, I'm really grateful. It's terrific for me to have someone around like you, someone who's not all hidebound and petty, someone I can really talk to as an equal, who understands what I'm on about.'

She was saying all the right things and Madeleine, predictably, glowed.

'But,' asked Laura, still solicitous, 'are you sure it's OK? It is enormously kind of you, but are you sure you're not going to mind having us around?'

'It'll be no problem,' said Madeleine, 'because I am going to be away for that weekend.'

'So you mean we can have the house to ourselves?' Laura tried not to let her grin become too huge. It wouldn't do to show how much more she relished the prospect of being alone with her lover, without her aunt emoting around the place. 'Oh, what a pity. Then you won't meet Terry. I'm sure the two of you would have lots in common,' she lied.

'Yes, you can have the house for the weekend.' Then, to show that she hadn't quite forgiven her niece's treatment of her gift-horse, Madeleine added, 'Or for as much of the weekend as Terry's mother can spare him.'

'Don't worry. We'll sort that out.' Laura was confident now; the prospect of having the free run of Madeleine's house with her lover had cheered her enormously.

'Good,' Madeleine smiled beatifically at her niece. 'There is one thing, of course.'

'What?'

'You'd better not tell Aggie that I won't be there.'

Laura's hand leapt to her mouth in mock-horror. 'Good Lord, no. Yes, she's hardly going to believe that I'm staying with you if she knows you're away.'

'Exactly.'

'Is she likely to find out?'

'Only if you tell her, Laura.'

The girl winked. 'Your secret is safe with me.' She grinned. 'So, in fact, while you're providing an alibi for me, I will also be providing an alibi for you.'

Madeleine laughed her silvery laugh. 'Sounds a bit over-dramatic, but I suppose you could see it like that.'

Laura looked into her aunt's eyes. 'Why? What are *you* up to that weekend?'

'Ah,' said Madeleine, retaining her mystery. 'Wouldn't you like to know?'

She had always liked intrigue, and being involved in this conspiracy with Bernard gave her a positive charge of excitement. It refurbished her old fantasy of Madeleine Severn, the *femme fatale,* and imparted drama to every preparation that she made for the encounter at Winter Jasmine Cottage. It made her feel special.

After the lunch with Laura, she returned to Kemp Town to change into her disguise.

She put on black tights, an old black, shapeless T-shirt dress which she had ceased to wear some couple of years before, and boring black shoes which had been discarded soon after purchase as unsuitable to the style of Madeleine Severn. Over these she belted a black coat which had been her mother's and which was usually aired only at funerals.

The red-gold hair that was her glory must, of course, be hidden. She shaped it into a tight bun on the back of her head and over this placed a large black beret, which she occasionally affected when her hair was loose, but had never before used for concealment. However, it served the purpose admirably.

Then, gilding the lily perhaps, she put on a pair of black-rimmed sunglasses she had bought when on an art-appreciation package-tour to Venice two years previously. As she did so, she felt a stray hair snag on a roughness on her hand. She looked with dismay at her knuckles, to see the creases in the skin looking dry and chalky. One or two had split, to show a moist redness inside. Both hands were similarly affected.

The sight angered her. She recognised

immediately what it was, a skin infection which affected her in times of emotional upheaval. It had appeared once or twice during her teens, erupted quite virulently in the months surrounding John Kaczmarek's death, but since then had not troubled her. For the infection to appear now, when she had a new lover, when she wanted to look her best, was aggravating in the extreme.

She would get some cream from the chemist. Maybe there was something new on the market that would clear it up before it got any worse. For the time being, she added a pair of gloves to her black ensemble.

She cast a final look in the mirror and decided that no one would recognise her. This was probably true, though whether the costume made her inconspicuous was another question. The casual observer might have been forgiven for thinking she was playing the part of a spy in an amateur dramatic society production.

She went to the local chemist, where she knew the proprietor well. He took a look at her hands and produced a recently-developed steroid-based cream which was supposed to be very good. If that didn't sort it out in a week, he said, she'd better go and see her doctor; skin conditions were funny things. Madeleine rubbed some of the cream on to the affected areas, replaced her gloves, caught a bus to Brighton Station and took the next train up to Victoria.

She knew exactly where she wanted to go. Victoria Line to Green Park, Piccadilly Line to Covent Garden. Thence a quick walk to Laura Ashley in Bow Street.

She chose the sheets and pillow-cases first. Her pastoral image of country cottages demanded a white or cream background and some floral or herbal design.

From the considerable selection, she homed in on a pattern of green and brown sprigs from some unidentified plant set against a background the colour of milky coffee. The design seemed right, rustic and yet at the same time smart, reminiscent of shepherdesses (or perhaps of Marie Antoinettes playing at shepherdesses).

She then turned her attention to the nightdress. This, though a more important purchase, was easier to find, because she had such a distinct image of what she required. She quickly selected one in white linen, with a high, chastely frilled neck and a pleated panel coming down to just below the breasts. She held it against herself, looked in a mirror and was satisfied that it looked properly sacrificial.

The uninterested girl at the counter said, as she keyed the information into the cash-register, 'Right, one nightdress, one pair single sheets, one pair—'

'Single?' Madeleine repeated. 'But I wanted double.'

'Well, you got single.'

'I'll just go and change them.'

The girl sighed truculently at this disruption, and Madeleine had to join the end of the queue after exchanging the sheets. When her turn came again, she was greeted by a sarcastic, 'Got it right this time, have you?' from the girl on the cash-register.

Madeleine did not deign to reply.

'How do you want to pay?'

'Cash.' She had thought this out and withdrawn a large amount of money over the last few days. Deep in her Mata Hari dream, she did not want to reveal her identity by cheques or credit cards.

The girl was no more interested in how Madeleine paid than in anything else about her, and the purchases were made.

When she emerged into the street, Madeleine looked at her watch. It was after five. She had no desire to hurry to Victoria and become embroiled in the rush-hour.

She wandered round the piazzas of Covent Garden, looking idly at the shops and stalls. She bought a copper hair-slide in the shape of a leaf. Then she meandered off, still killing time, with the vague intention of catching a tube at Oxford Circus. She felt unpressured and happy. There was no itching from her hands; when the gloves were removed, she felt confident the skin would have cleared up. She looked in shop-windows, watched the people, felt invisible in her black disguise.

By chance, her route took her to Wardour Street and then along a little alley that ran off it. She did not notice the doorway which still bore the bell-pushes for 'Mandy' and 'Cleo'. She did not know of the fate of the former, which had only had scant coverage in the national press.

Nor did she know that police investigations had not yet discovered the identity of the prostitute's murderer. They had found few clues, but were working on the theory that the killing was one of a series that had taken place over the previous five years.

16

'For Christ's sake!' said Tony Ashton, rolling off Sharon on the sofa of her sitting-room. 'I mean, come on. You can't hold out for ever. Look, you want it—God knows I want it—let's just get on and do it, for Christ's sake.'

Sharon smiled sweetly and started to button up her blouse. 'We've been through this before, Tony, and I still feel exactly the same about it. I am not going to make love to you. I am not going to make love to anyone before I'm married.'

'But why, for Christ's sake? This is the bloody eighties. Virginity went out some time back in the fifties.'

'Not for me, Tony.'

'Oh, but come on, how much longer do you think I'm going to go around with you when I'm not getting any? There are other girls I know who aren't quite so

227

bloody scared of sex.'

'I'm not scared of it,' Sharon repeated patiently. 'I just think it's something that belongs with marriage.'

'Well, if I never ring you up again, you'll know the reason.' He stood up defiantly.

'Yes, I will. And I'll be very sad. You mean a lot to me, Tony. I don't want to lose you.'

He clenched his fists. 'For Christ's sake, you don't *have* to lose me. All you got to do is let me make love to you. It'll be all right— I won't get you in the club or anything.'

Sharon shook her head firmly. 'I'm sorry, Tony.'

He shook his head and sat down, deflated, in an armchair.

There was a silence before Sharon spoke again. 'I was talking to Dad the other day. . . .' Tony made no response. 'About the pub. He said he's always looking for bar staff.'

'Oh yes?' It was said with complete lack of interest.

'That's how he started. You work in the bar, if you're good, you get given more responsibility, then after a time you become a manager, do that well you can get your own pub. That's what Dad did.'

'So bloody what?'

'Tony, all I was thinking was—you haven't got a job, maybe you might—'

'Now listen, sweetheart,' he snapped, pointing an angry finger at her, 'if and when I ever do get a job, it's not going to be as a bloody barman!'

'No. All right. Just an idea.'

'Forget it,' said Tony. But he didn't say it with quite the same vehemence as when she had last mentioned the idea. Sharon thought she might be beginning to get somewhere.

'Dad'll be back soon. If you wanted to have a word with him. . . .'

'I don't want to have a bloody word with him,' said Tony, separating each word with venomous clarity. 'I'm going.' He slouched towards the door.

'You'll call me?' asked Sharon.

'I wouldn't bloody count on it,' he said, as he walked out.

But Sharon did count on it, and Tony knew he would be in touch with her again. He was confused and angered by the effect she had on him. God, he wasn't even getting any bloody sex, for Christ's sake! If his mates ever found out, they'd laugh their bloody arses off. But, in spite of that, he would be in touch with her again.

Sharon went up to have a bath, content with her evening's work. She still did want him enormously, but she had managed to control her lust, and now she felt she was beginning to control Tony too. He wasn't an ideal candidate for her plans, but he could be moulded. If she could organise him into a job—particularly in her father's business—Tony would cease to be quite such a ridiculous contender for the main part in her main fantasy. She'd have to get rid of the ear-ring, of course, and she'd have to change his attitudes towards jobs and mortgages, but she didn't think any of it was beyond the realms of possibility.

Tony Ashton did not know that he was observed leaving Sharon's house. Paul Grigson sat slumped over the wheel of his mother's car, with a new bone-handled sheathknife on his belt. He had felt naked after Madeleine confiscated the black one, and replaced it from the same shop on his way home the same day.

The sense of power he got from having

the knife was diminishing, but driving the car gave it new strength. His mother was still being kept in hospital and she need never know that her Mini was being used. He was taking a big risk, of course, driving around before he had passed his test, but the danger excited him.

What was happening with his mother he didn't know. He went to see her every day or so and she seemed to look much the same each time. Maybe a little thinner, but not dramatically so. He didn't talk to her about what was actually wrong, but was told each time that she would have to stay in the hospital a little longer. He knew he should ask the ward-sister or one of the doctors about her illness, but something in him didn't want it defined.

In the meantime, he lived in limbo, camping out untidily at home, eating unheated food out of tins, wearing unironed shirts more days than he should. But the chaos of his domestic arrangements was nothing to the chaos in his mind, where constantly shifting desires and memories took ever more threatening forms.

He only used the car after dark, as if the night gave him a cloak of invisibility. Some of the time he just drove around aimlessly, but he spent hours parked within sight of Madeleine's front door, watching to see who came and went. That evening he had been there for a couple of hours, until he had seen a black-clad figure, whose outline he knew to be Madeleine's, return to the house at about nine o'clock. He had continued his vigil until the downstairs lights went off and the upstairs ones went on. Then there had seemed no point in staying.

Driving home via Sharon's house and parking outside there had been an act of sheer masochism, turning the knife in another of his wounds. And seeing Tony Ashton emerging from the house with his customary cocksure gait had only confirmed Paul's sense of his own inferiority.

For a moment he contemplated driving after his rival, running him down perhaps, leaping out of the car and attacking him. His hand tightened on the bone handle of the new knife.

But then it relaxed. The dream of violence passed and he let Tony Ashton walk off, unmolested, down the street.

Tony Ashton wasn't his real enemy. Paul had never really cared about Sharon. His pain had derived only from the public shame of his virginity.

No, it was Madeleine he really cared about, and his real enemy was his rival for her.

Bernard Hopkins had become the focus for all Paul's images of violence. And in his mind, the setting for that violence had also become fixed.

It was Winter Jasmine Cottage, Shorton, near Pulborough.

17

Madeleine had devoted the Thursday evening to her packing. It was only a weekend, but it was an important weekend and she was determined to get all the set-dressing right. The climax, bed, had been catered for by the sheets and the white nightdress, but there were other moments during a weekend of love for which she knew she must be properly prepared.

There was the dinner *à deux* beforehand, and for that she selected a long black dress with full, hanging sleeves. It was cut rather on the lines of something that Guinevere might have worn when mourning King Arthur. To complement this, she chose a long belt of plaited silver which could be tied loosely and allowed to dangle, reinforcing the medieval image. Her hair, she decided, would be displayed to best advantage gathered loosely at the nape with her silver brooch shaped like a Highland shield. This could be easily unclasped at the right moment, to allow the full red-gold glory to cascade down over her shoulders.

She also needed day-clothes, lighter garments for lazing side by side before the open fire, thicker, fuzzier jumpers to cocoon her as they took long country walks, arms linked, safe in the togetherness of their love. She selected some of her usual skirts and pullovers in their customary muted hues. She was concerned to show how natural she was, how unaffected, how little effort she was making. Bernard must take her as she was.

Each time she thought of Bernard she felt a little *frisson,* part pure excitement, part fear. The surrender of her virginity was not something she was taking lightly. The eczema on her hands, which the chemist's cream had not cleared up, was a constant reminder of just how seriously she was taking it. She remembered, uneasily, awkwardnesses with other men, her reactions to former passes, the way she had recoiled from their touch. But then none of the other men had been right. The thought of Bernard calmed her. He was so sensitive, so well-read, so gentle. Everything would be all right with Bernard.

When she had packed her suitcase, she laid out her travelling clothes. Once again she homed in on the black ensemble she had worn for her shopping expedition. And she was going to need gloves, no question about that. All right, if they had to be worn, she would jolly well make a feature of them. She took a pair of elbow-length black gloves out of a drawer. They struck her as wonderfully dramatic, a touch of chic, accessories for a *femme fatale* from a forties Hollywood movie.

When her wardrobe was complete, she went downstairs to put the final touches to the weekend's food. Most of it had been prepared well in advance and deposited in the freezer—leek and potato soup, a lasagne, a chicken curry. She would buy fresh vegetables for interesting salads on the Friday. She had also made sweets, a *galette*, Dutch apple tart, hazelnut meringue. While wishing to demonstrate to Bernard how natural she was, she did not intend to miss another opportunity of showing off her domestic skills.

Finally, she chose some books to take

with her for the weekend. Just one or two, casually picked out, things she just happened to be reading or rereading at the time. After half an hour of browsing, she settled on *Wuthering Heights*, the Everyman edition of Webster and Turner's *Selected Plays* and *The Poems of Emily Dickinson*. The selection seemed appropriately random.

She decided to put the books in the brief-case that she took to work. She would take that along with her. It seemed right to stress the seriousness with which she approached her teaching, and the brief-case, with its jumble of notes, essays, books and other oddments, was an excellent expression of her essentially feminine intelligence.

Madeleine woke early on the Friday morning, fluttery with anticipation. She put clean sheets on the double-bed in the spare room in preparation for Laura and Terry. Then she checked through her packing again.

She had had minimal contact with Bernard during the last week. Now the tryst was established, they did not need to risk unnecessary communication. Madeleine was increasingly aware of the shadowy presence of Shirley Hopkins.

Bernard had told Madeleine his alibi. So far as his wife was concerned, he was at a weekend conference on language teaching at a London hotel. He did not seem worried about the subterfuge. But what, Madeleine had asked, if his wife should ring the hotel to contact him? There was no danger of that, he said. Shirley was going to her mother's for the weekend. It would be all right.

As the assignation approached, Bernard's confidence seemed to grow. His certainty, on the few occasions they spoke, comforted Madeleine, and allayed her own misgivings.

She had a class at the Garrettway on the Friday morning. Paul Grigson in for a revision session on romantic poetry, to see, as the date of the Oxford entrance examinations approached, whether he had taken in any of the stuff she had been teaching him over the last few weeks. The answer seemed to be that he had assimilated little. His concentration was bad, he was unable to recall the simplest details of what they had covered, and he was tongue-tied when she questioned him.

Madeleine also noticed that the boy looked a mess. There was a grubbiness about him.

His shirt collar was wrinkled with dirt and he needed a shave. On another occasion Madeleine might have asked if anything was the matter, might have shown again her wonderful understanding of young people, and re-established the mother-and-child intimacy which she and the boy had previously achieved. But she was too preoccupied that morning to have sympathy to share.

At the end of the class she set two subjects for revision essays and, gathering her papers, hurried out of the room before him.

So she did not see the expression of pain, disappointment and fury with which the boy's eyes followed her.

Madeleine picked up a couple of rolls from the wholefood shop and set off on the route she normally took when in an emotional state. Walks along the sea-front were always her recourse in times of stress.

It was surprisingly warm for November. The watery sunlight glowed on her cheeks and made her feel immediately better. The forecast had been good; it would be a fine weekend. That seemed propitious. As she walked along the front, her confidence returned.

She was special, a woman with a secret. The people who walked past her did not give her a second glance. They did not know that she was about to spend a weekend with her lover, they did not know the strength of passion within her. She was Madeleine Severn, whose beauty could drive men mad.

She felt a new reality about herself, as if she were suddenly part of everything she had ever read. She and Bernard would match the greatest lovers of fiction. They would be together for ever. She would bear his child.

The thought settled her. Her customary sense of well-being returned, and Madeleine Severn felt it glowing around her like an aura as she walked along the Brighton front.

'I'm very glad,' Aggie whispered to her sister over a cup of tea in the kitchen, 'that Laura's spending the weekend with you.'

'Nice for me too,' said Madeleine with a diplomatic smile.

'At least at weekends I know she can't be with this man.'

'The boyfriend?'

'Yes. He's not around at weekends, thank goodness.'

'Why do you disapprove of him so strongly?'

'Oh, I don't disapprove of him that much. There's nothing really wrong with him. It's just that he's too old, and Laura's too young.' Aggie avoided her sister's eyes as she said this. Both of them knew they were thinking back to what had happened to her when she was seventeen.

'Laura has to grow up sometime,' Madeleine suggested gently. She was back on an even keel now; she had sympathy and wisdom once again to share with the world.

'But not yet,' insisted Aggie. Madeleine shrugged. 'Yes, I know it has to happen. I know I'm being a clinging mother. I just. . . .' But she couldn't define what she was trying to say. 'Anyway, I'm glad she's going to be with you. If you get a chance to talk a little sense into her. . . .'

'I'll do what I can,' said Madeleine in a worldly-wise voice that implied she was not very optimistic of success. Fully aware of her duplicity as she spoke, and receiving a sense of power from it, she continued,

'What are you and Keith doing over the weekend?'

'Oh, not a lot. The other two are staying with friends. Be nice for us to have the house to ourselves for a change.'

Mindful of Laura's analysis of Keith and Aggie's marriage, Madeleine had a clear idea of how they might use this unaccustomed privacy, but she put the thought from her mind. Some things she preferred not to think about, and the idea that there was any comparison between Keith and Aggie's activities and what was to take place between Bernard and herself that night at Winter Jasmine Cottage was distasteful to her.

At that point Laura came downstairs, changed from work and carrying a small overnight case. It did not occur to her mother that the girl was perhaps overdressed and overperfumed for a weekend with her aunt.

As goodbyes were being said, Madeleine took her niece's hand and, again delighting in the deception, began to catalogue all the nice things that the two of them were going to do over the weekend. Laura found this detail excessive, but played along.

Keith was sitting in the front room, reading, as he had been for the past half-hour, a copy of the *Sun*. Madeleine restrained herself, as she always had to, from asking how anyone could spend more than five minutes on that newspaper, and said goodbye.

Keith nodded awkwardly and, without getting up from the sofa (as Madeleine knew Bernard would have done), mumbled, 'Cheerio.'

As they walked through the darkness to Madeleine's green Renault 5, she hissed to her niece, 'See. No problem.'

'No,' said Laura, with less certainty.

'Something wrong? Are you worried about deceiving them?'

Laura dismissed that idea with a toss of her head. 'No, it's Terry. I told you he goes back to Worcester at weekends.'

'You mean he can't come?'

'No, he's coming, but just for tonight. His Mum's had a bit of a setback, so he's got to drive up to Worcester in the morning.'

'Oh. Well, at least you'll have tonight.'

Laura nodded ruefully. 'Yes.' Then, remembering that she hoped the weekend's exercise was going to set a precedent, she quickly added, 'Please don't think I'm ungrateful for what you're doing. I was only thinking, I'm going to be just stuck in the house on my own most of the weekend. Unless you're going to be back earlier. . . ?'

Madeleine shook her head. 'Sunday evening.'

'Are you going to tell me now where you're going?' asked Laura, teasing.

'We all have our secrets,' replied Madeleine enigmatically.

They got into the car and set off. It was dark and there was quite a lot of traffic about, so they did not notice the parked Mini which came to life as they left and followed them down to the other end of town.

Madeleine was very solicitous to Laura when they reached the house. She showed her the spare bed with its clean sheets and then, downstairs, opened the freezer to reveal the food for Laura and Terrys' weekend.

Laura was touchingly grateful for her aunt's generosity, and Madeleine received a thrill from being thanked as Pandarus by someone unaware that her true role for the weekend was that of Cressida. Romantic intrigue, she decided, suited her.

Just before seven, she announced that she must go. Terry was expected round half-past, and Madeleine said she didn't want to be around when he arrived. 'I'm sure you'd rather just be the two of you.'

Laura, lying, denied this.

Madeleine picked up a small flight-bag, kissed her niece tenderly, and said goodbye.

Laura looked up mischievously, and tried once again. 'So I still don't get to find out where you're going?'

'I,' said Madeleine, 'am going nowhere. I am staying here alone with you, Laura. Just as you are staying here alone with me.' She opened her eyes wide to an expression of mock-innocence. 'And if anyone asks either of us about this weekend, that's what we tell them.'

Madeleine was still dressed in her normal clothes when she left the house. Her 'disguise' was in the flight-bag.

She got into the Renault 5 and drove up to park near the Garrettway School of Languages. As a trusted member of staff, she had a key to the building, and let herself in. She did not notice the Mini which was parking a little way up the street.

Once inside the school, Madeleine went

to the ladies room, because it had a large mirror. There she took off her outer garments and tights, keeping on the new underwear which she had put on before going to collect Laura. She changed quickly into her black ensemble, then, checking in the mirror, pushed her hair back under the beret and put on the dark glasses. She kept on her ordinary driving-gloves over her raw hands; the moment for the forties-heroine look would come later. Folding up her everyday clothes, she put them in the flight-bag. One last look in the mirror, then she switched off the light and stepped out into the hall.

She had taken two steps when she heard the click of a key in the front-door lock.

She froze in the darkness. The door opened, spilling a slice of light from the streetlamps. It opened further to outline the figure of a man. His hand reached to the light-switch.

Madeleine blinked in the sudden brightness, as she heard a familiar voice demand, 'Who the hell are you? What are you doing here?'

It was Julian Garrett. Behind him stood a blonde girl in her late teens.

There was nothing for it. Madeleine had to take the glasses and beret off. 'It's only me, Julian. I left some papers that I needed over the weekend.'

He looked at her ironically, taking in her unusual costume. But he didn't challenge her, just said in a tone that implied complicity in their lies, 'I was coming in to give this young lady a tutorial.'

'Ah. Well, I've got my stuff, so I'd better be off,' said Madeleine.

Julian stood aside and, with a sardonic smile on his lips, watched her out of the building.

Madeleine felt only a little flustered as she got into her car. Meeting Julian had been unfortunate, but not disastrous. He might suspect that she was up to something, but he would never guess what.

She switched on the interior light and readjusted the beret in the rear-view mirror. She discarded the glasses when she found she could hardly see anything in the dark. Even without them, she felt confident of her disguise.

It didn't occur to her that the disguise was pretty useless as long as she was driving her own car.

And it certainly didn't occur to her that lights of the car which followed her Renault all the way to Pulborough belonged to a Mini driven by one of her pupils.

18

Paul had bought a half-bottle of whisky and kept swigging at it to calm the trembling in his body. After a time the alcohol made him feel detached, as though he were floating a few feet in the air above the Mini. He no longer worried about his driving; he was in control—in fact, he was driving better than he usually did. The drink had dissolved his inhibitions.

He kept about five car-lengths behind the green Renault. Every now and then another car passed him and intervened between them, but Madeleine was not driving fast, so she too was quickly overtaken and their proximity restored. Paul was not worried that she might notice she was being tailed. He felt reckless now. If she realised what was happening, then she realised. It didn't matter. The fact that he was driving illegally didn't matter either. The only thing that mattered was that he would be with Madeleine that night.

After the confusion and wild, alarming images of the previous days, Paul's fantasies had now crystallised into an unchanging picture. Its details were still obscure, but the outline was clear. Bernard and Madeleine had arranged to spend the weekend together at Winter Jasmine Cottage, but Bernard was not going to make it. Paul would take his place. Madeleine did not love Bernard. She loved Paul, and she must be made to realise that. And she only would realise it when Bernard was out of the way. Then she would recognise her true feelings. They would fall into each other's arms. They would go to bed together. She would be very gentle, and the great burden would be lifted from him. Thereafter they would never part.

Paul felt the car pulling towards the verge and took another swig from the whisky-bottle to steady himself. He blinked, but the tail-lights of the green Renault were still ahead of him.

It was all easy, and it would continue to be easy. Even if he lost sight of Madeleine's car, it would not matter. He knew where she was going. If he had to, he would find

Winter Jasmine Cottage without her guidance. Nothing could change what was going to happen. He gripped the steering-wheel fiercely, forcing himself to concentrate on his driving.

And he felt the comforting hardness of the bone-handled sheath-knife on his belt pressing against the back of the car-seat.

19

Bernard had had a class with his Italians until six, and after that he did not travel directly from Brighton to Winter Jasmine Cottage. It was a little out of his way, but he had decided to go there via his home in Henfield. He had left some champagne in the fridge and there were a few other bits and pieces he wanted to collect.

He knew the house would be empty when he got there, and he was whistling as he parked the Austin Maxi and let himself in. He felt confident now; his guilts and anxieties had dissipated as the weekend drew nearer. He was doing the right thing. Madeleine was the right person and he was behaving in the only way possible for him.

First he went out to the garden shed where some red roses were standing in a bucket of water. He shook the moisture off their stems and carefully replaced the cellophane packaging in which he had bought them earlier in the day. He wondered whether there would be a vase at the cottage and, deciding it would be better to be safe than sorry, looked out the old cut-glass one his mother had always used as a centre-piece for the dinner-table.

His suitcase was already packed and he took it out from under the bed. Still whistling, he went into the bathroom to prepare his sponge-bag. He felt his chin and decided that he would do better to shave again. When he had finished, he massaged some after-shave on to the smooth skin and packed his shaving tackle. He looked at his face in the mirror. The brown eyes that returned his stare were mature, confident, and loved.

In the bedroom he opened the top drawer of the dressing-table. He moved back a pile of underwear to reveal a couple of old packets of Durex which had been there for some time. He hesitated briefly, before making his decision and putting the packets into his sponge-bag. He unzipped the top of his case and put in the sponge-bag. Then he took the case downstairs.

In the kitchen he took out some old

newspapers from the cupboard where they were kept and wrapped them round the two bottles of champagne he had taken out of the fridge. There were another four bottles in the car, but those would have plenty of time to chill at Winter Jasmine Cottage. He had checked with Mrs Waterstone that there was a fridge. It was only for dinner that evening that he needed the cold ones. He secured the newspapers round the bottles with thick rubber bands.

He stood still for a minute and went through a mental check-list of all the things that he had needed to do before leaving. Yes, all the details seemed to have been covered.

All except one. He had one more thing to do and then he could set off, the third fantasy converging on the reality of Winter Jasmine Cottage.

20

Madeleine did not notice the police car drawn up at the roadside just outside Pulborough. She was a prudent driver who always kept within speed limits, so the police held no fears for her, anyway. As the Renault approached the town's thirty-mile-an-hour limit, she slowed down, a fact that the two constables in the Rover noted with approval. But they took little notice of her; law-abiding drivers held no interest for them.

The Mini that was following, however, did merit their attention. The untidiness with which it slowed down after her alerted them, as did its wobbling course across the road. The police driver nodded to his companion and the white car slid out in pursuit.

Paul's vision was blurred and it took him a few moments to identify the source of the flashing lights. Eventually he found the rear-view mirror and managed to focus on the car behind. He saw the whiteness and, as it passed under a street-lamp, the blue dome of the light on top. The headlights continued to flash, obviously urging him to stop.

He only hesitated for a moment before pushing down his foot hard on the accelerator and swinging out to overtake Madeleine. He didn't have to keep behind her. He knew the address. He could find her.

An oncoming vehicle made him cut in sharply, causing Madeleine to brake. The police car's blue light and siren were switched on. When the oncoming car was cleared, the police driver accelerated and pulled out to overtake the Renault. Madeleine tutted and continued driving at twenty-seven miles an hour as the police car surged ahead.

Paul's foot was flat down on the accelerator, but the Mini hadn't as much power as the Rover behind him. He twitched at the steering-wheel to negotiate a roundabout, made too wide a circle and mounted the kerb. By the time he had righted himself, the police car was even closer. He kept his foot down, but the Rover pulled out and drew alongside. The constable in the passenger-seat was waving him down.

Still he kept going, so the police car surged ahead until it was in front of the Mini, and slowed down. Paul tried to pull out to overtake, but there was a car coming down from the opposite direction, fast. He had no alternative. He braked and stopped the car.

Both policemen got out and came towards the Mini, one on either side. The one nearer Paul indicated that he should wind down his window. 'In rather a hurry, aren't you?' he said, without humour.

Paul nodded, trying desperately to think what he should do next. The policeman sniffed and looked across at the passenger-seat where the half-bottle of whisky caught the gleam from a street-lamp. 'Have you been drinking?' he asked. 'I'm afraid I'm going to have to ask you—'

But he didn't get out the rest of the sentence. Paul, who had not switched off the engine, slammed the car back into gear, and accelerated again. The policeman leapt aside as the Mini jumped forward.

Paul jerked the wheel to the right and pulled out around the police car. There were oncoming headlights close, very close. He swung the wheel wildly and the Mini, missing the other vehicle by a whisker, careered across to the opposite side of the road and came to rest with its right-hand wing buried in a street-lamp. The driver of the other vehicle brought his car to an untidy stop as the two policemen moved vengefully across towards the immobilised Mini

At that moment Madeleine's Renault 5 caught up with them. She noted with disapproval that there had been an accident and pulled out cautiously to go round the stationary Rover. She was aware that the two constables were helping someone out of the Mini, but she could not see who it was. She drove on towards Winter Jasmine Cottage.

Paul was shaken, but not seriously hurt. The car had not been going very fast at the moment of impact.

'Now what the hell do you think you're playing at?' demanded the policeman he had nearly run down.

'I'm in a hurry,' said Paul, the words loose and slurring on his tongue.

'We could see that,' said the constable grimly. 'Is this your car?'

'It's my mother's.'

'Oh yes? Can I see your licence?'

'Look, I'm in a hurry,' Paul was suddenly desperate. 'I'm in a hurry! I've got to go somewhere!'

The policeman shook his head implacably. 'No, son,' he said. 'You aren't going anywhere tonight.'

21

Bernard paused for a moment in his bed-room before he changed his clothes, and thought about his wife. Would it have been better, he wondered, not for the first time, if he had not told Madeleine he was married? Might their relationship have been freer, less inhibited by secrecy and guilt? His feelings for Madeleine were so strong, so well-defined, that their affair should not be limited by outside considerations.

But, even as he thought this, he felt relieved that his wife had been mentioned. It was better to proceed cautiously at first. The existence of an ailing wife in the background gave him a kind of security. If things didn't work out with Madeleine, he would have an excuse for ending the relationship: his conscience could not cope with the strains of duplicity. And if his love for Madeleine developed as he hoped it would, then there were many, simple ways of disposing of Shirley Hopkins.

He was not ungrateful to her. She had taken the pressure off him on many occasions. The fact that people knew him to be married had frequently saved awkwardness, and the fact that his wife was crippled had prevented curious probings into his private life. People were so bloody nosey, so prurient, it was difficult to keep any secrets. But respect for his sick wife had kept everyone at a distance from Bernard; colleagues from work had not come to visit him at home; a few had suggested social engagements, but he had always had the excuse of his wife's infirmity to make polite refusals. He had used the excuse in all his previous employments during the last five years, the seven other teaching jobs he had had before Garrettway.

Shirley explained so much about Bernard. She explained his shyness, his lack of sociability, his unwillingness to mix with people outside a work environment. She answered unspoken questions about his sexual nature; she made him a respectable eunuch. People thought (as Stella Franklin had): Poor man, he must have all the normal masculine urges and yet he's saddled with a crippled wife; he can't have much of a sex life, it must be very difficult for him. And, having reached that conclusion, the curious then put him from their minds and asked no further questions. Which was exactly what Bernard wanted.

Shirley was, in fact, the ideal partner for him. It was the perfect relationship.

So long as he didn't fall in love with someone else. It was then that his security was threatened. There had been other women before Madeleine, affairs that had nearly started, but which had failed and from which he had escaped, using the excuse of Shirley. And, though each skirmish had left him confused, frightened and exhausted, he had on each occasion managed to drag himself back to sanity, to reassert the *status quo*.

But none of the other women had affected him as Madeleine did. For the first time in his life, at an age when he had almost written off the possibility, Bernard Hopkins had fallen in love and, though he tried to argue against it, he knew that this was the affair he had to see through. Madeleine offered him a chance of catching up on all his lost opportunities, of living a normal life, and in those circumstances his relationship with Shirley became irrelevant.

It would no longer work. If things turned out well with Madeleine, Bernard would not need Shirley. And, her value as an excuse gone, the existence of a wife slowly succumbing to multiple sclerosis would become nothing more than an embarrassment. He would have to get rid of her.

But not yet. See how the weekend with Madeleine went. Keep the options open. Bernard had learned by experience to be prudent, not to rush into things. He might still need Shirley, and his wife might once again have to provide the excuse for which he had invented her.

The idea had come to him suddenly when being interviewed for his first new job after his mother's death five years before. The principal of that particular language school had asked if he was married and the affirmative answer came out instinctively. Once the lie had been perpetrated, Bernard recognised its advantages and began to add to it.

The name had been the first embellishment. Shirley, his mother's name, had come automatically to his mind. And, from the moment she had been christened, the new Shirley Hopkins showed her worth. From the start, she protected her husband from speculation. But then a colleague asked him to come to dinner *with his wife,* and Bernard, again instinctively, had had to invent Shirley's illness. As his creation grew and developed, he found increasingly that she helped to fill the void his beloved mother's death had left in him.

Bernard Hopkins looked around the bedroom of the house where he had lived all his life, with both parents till his father's death fifteen years before, then with his mother until she too had died, ten years later. And since that time, alone.

He looked at the single bed in which he had slept all his life. He looked at the clothes laid out on it. He felt calm now, as he slowly undressed. And calm as he put on the brown herring-bone sports jacket and dark grey flannel trousers which had belonged to his father, and which Bernard Hopkins had worn for the killings of four prostitutes, the most recent of whom had been called 'Mandy'.

22

Madeleine knew that she was likely to arrive at Winter Jasmine Cottage before Bernard. He had told her of his class with the Italians and given her Mrs Waterstone's instructions about the key under the water-butt. It suited her well to be there first. She could look around, start their dinner, make up the bed, change into her black dress, maybe add a few little feminine touches to the place, be welcoming when Bernard arrived.

She drove with care down the rutted track from the main road. She might have missed the little turning off to the cottage but for the very specific instructions Bernard had given her. It felt later than it was; there had hardly been any traffic since Pulborough. It was a dark night, but her headlights already caught the sparkle of frost on the ground, which was hard and dry. There had been no rain for ten days.

All she felt now was excitement. The fear had gone, leaving only a flutter of anticipation inside her. She was secure in her disguise, secure in her alibi. Madeleine Severn was driving to meet her lover.

She gripped the steering-wheel with her gloved hands and peered ahead as the laurel hedge appeared in her headlights. The Renault 5 turned in through the entrance and stopped on the crisp gravel so that the full beam illuminated Winter Jasmine Cottage. It was perfect—small, old and beautiful. Her fantasies could not have provided a better setting for her sacrifice.

Even in November, Winter Jasmine Cottage looked comforting; in the summer it must be heavenly. A new fantasy started to grow in her mind, of the two of them living permanently somewhere like this, working together in the garden on long hot afternoons, hearing the calls of birds and the cheerful cries of children.

She took a torch from the glove compartment and stepped out of the car. The coldness of the air stung her cheeks. The night was absolutely silent. There was no distant hum of traffic, and no birds sang. The crunch of her shoes on the gravel sounded unnaturally loud.

It was a lonely place, but it did not frighten her. On the contrary, its isolation felt so right that it made her even more excited. Here was somewhere outside normal life; it fitted exactly the specifications she had mentioned to Bernard: 'somewhere magical, somewhere private, that's just for us.' She recalled that when she had first said this, she had followed it with the quotation from Marvell,

'The grave's a fine and private place,
But none, I think, do there embrace.'

The idea seemed funny and she giggled aloud in the darkness. It was so wonderful to know that she would soon be with Bernard, someone who understood her literary allusions, someone who could complete quotations for her, someone who was intellectually as well as physically compatible. At last the man had been found who would complement the infinite variety of Madeleine Severn.

The torch-beam found the water-butt. It was propped up on bricks, so she had no difficulty in reaching underneath for the key. She went round to the front door and opened Winter Jasmine Cottage.

The light, when switched on, revealed that the door opened straight into the living-room, though there was a curtain on a rail to act as a draught-excluder. The cottage's interior also matched Madeleine's fantasies. The living-room was small, with chintzy curtains drawn back from diamond-paned windows. It was dominated by a large fireplace, which took up most of one wall. In front of this two armchairs were cosily spaced. They were covered in material with a design of pheasants on it, worn but not shabby. Behind them was a small dining-table with two chairs. Everything seemed to be planned for two. On the walls hung a selection of paintings, glassware and wood-carvings, souvenirs from the Waterstones' holidays in Europe before the war. In one corner stood an old harmonium with faded purple silk panels. The ceiling was low and bisected by a black, uneven beam.

The first thing Madeleine did was to close the curtains. The tiny room at once became more intimate. Then she turned her attention to the fireplace, and found that Mrs Rankin, the lady who looked after the cot-

268

tage between lets, had done her job well. In the wrought-iron basket-grate a fire was laid, balls of newspaper surmounted by kindling and then logs of increasing size. A well-laid fire, all done according to the best girl guide principles. On the oak mantelpiece was a box of matches and a note reading: 'Logs in cupboard to left of fire.' Madeleine put a match to the newspaper, which immediately flared and set up an efficient crackle amongst the kindling. She opened the adjacent cupboard and found that, true to the note, it was stacked high with neatly symmetrical logs.

Before she went out to unload the car, Madeleine turned off the overhead light and switched on two table-lamps. Their softer glow, mingled with the flicker of the growing fire, was more aesthetically pleasing.

She managed to carry everything in one trip, the cool-box containing the food, her suitcase and her briefcase. She put them down in the living-room and went to investigate the kitchen.

This was again tiny, but well equipped. Mrs Waterstone, when deciding to let out the cottage, had invested in all the hardware that her tenants might expect, electric cooker, fridge, washing-machine, even a dish-washer. Madeleine put the chicken curry in the oven to warm up slowly and loaded the rest of the food into the fridge. Everything in the kitchen, she noted with satisfaction, was spotlessly clean.

Back in the living-room the fire was burning merrily, casting a deep orange glow on the white walls. Madeleine picked up her suitcase and brief-case and went through the white door with a black latch which opened on to the steep stairs.

The upper floor of Winter Jasmine Cottage comprised a small landing, an equally small bathroom and, between them, taking up most of the space, the bedroom, whose window looked out over the front garden. Madeleine drew the curtains, which had on them a design of honeysuckle, and turned her attention to the bed. It was a generously proportioned double-bed with a dark wooden headboard. On either side stood a table with a green-shaded lamp. She switched these on and turned off the overhead light. As it had downstairs, the lower lighting source made the atmosphere more intimate.

She realised that, considering the weather,

the room was remarkably warm, and saw that Mrs Rankin had switched on the electric heater under the window. On it was a polite note requesting tenants to turn off the power before they left.

The bed was made up with clean cream-coloured blankets, a beige eiderdown and a fringed brown bedcover. Madeleine noted approvingly how well this colour scheme would go with the Laura Ashley sheets and pillow-cases, as she opened her suitcase and took them out. They were still in their cellophane wrappers. She had not removed her driving gloves since coming in to the cottage and had difficulty in undoing the packaging.

Taking off the gloves, she looked at her hands. To her annoyance, she saw that the eczema (or whatever it was) had got worse. There were more cracks along her knuckles and inside them a sticky redness showed. She resisted the temptation to scratch. It was infuriating. Everything else was so perfect, and she had to get this. However right it felt and however cool she was trying to be about it, the adventure was taking its toll on her. Still, nothing she could do. Have to make the best of it. It was a small thing, after all. She got some of the cream she had bought from the chemist out of her sponge-bag and rubbed it optimistically onto the affected area. Then she returned to the sheets, but, finding her hands too slippery, put the gloves back on and managed to make the bed without difficulty.

She plumped up the pillows in their crisp new cases, folded back the top sheet and surveyed the effect. It was very satisfactory. She felt comforted by her good taste; the sheets couldn't have been more appropriate.

There was something missing, though. After a moment she realised what it was and took the new white nightdress out of her suitcase. She laid it across the right-hand side of the bed. She felt sure that Bernard would want to be on the left. She couldn't explain why; it was just an instinct, one of those things that lovers know about each other without asking.

She looked at her watch. It was nearly half-past eight. He would be arriving soon. She must get changed quickly, so that she was ready to greet him. She shook her hair out of the beret and removed the rest of her disguise, folding the garments neatly and placing them in her suitcase. Then she slipped on her black dress and, surveying herself in the mirror, prepared to tie the braided silver belt. A thought stopped her. Hair first—it wouldn't do to have loose hairs showing on the dress. She took it off again, sat in front of the mirror and started to brush the red-gold hair that was her chief glory. She had washed it that morning, calculating the time-lapse carefully. By evening she knew it would have lost its just-washed fluffiness but retain the gleam imparted by her herbal shampoo.

So it proved, and she brushed the hair into its customary artless abandon with considerable satisfaction. She reached for the silver Celtic clasp, and gathered the red-gold strands behind her nape in readiness. But she changed her mind. The moment for her hair to be released could come at some other point over the weekend. The image of Millais' *The Bridesmaid* came to her. For this evening, the first evening, the important evening, she would wear her hair loose.

She replaced the dress and adjusted the belt to a properly casual knot. She took off the gloves in which she had been driving. Then she drew out of her sponge-bag a spray of her distinctive flowery perfume, puffed a little behind her ears and onto her wrists. For a moment the giggly thought of spraying it elsewhere occurred to her, but she put it from her mind.

She pulled on her long forties-heroine gloves and stood back to get as full a picture as the small mirror would allow. Though she said it herself, she had to admit that she looked pretty stunning.

At that moment she heard the hum of an approaching vehicle. She drew back one of the honeysuckle curtains to see headlights swinging through the gap in the laurel hedge.

Perfect timing, she thought, as she went downstairs to welcome her lover. It was symptomatic of how the whole weekend would turn out. Everything was going to be all right.

'Ah, but here's one,' said Bernard. 'Here's one. I bet you don't know this.'

'Try me,' Madeleine grinned. The curry had been a success. So had the hazelnut meringue. They had just broached the second bottle of cold champagne. The red roses stood in a vase on the dresser. The lovers were playing literary games. Madeleine had everything she could possibly want from life.

' "A rose-red city—half as old as Time," ' Bernard quoted carefully.

'Well, it's very familiar. . . .'

He nodded agreement, waiting for her identification of the source.

'It refers to Petra, in, um . . .' she couldn't exactly remember where, 'in the Middle East.'

'Yes.'

'And I would say it's early nineteenth century. . . ?'

'Nineteenth century, anyway.'

'It sounds sort of reminiscent of 'Ozymandias', doesn't it?' She took a stab. 'It isn't Shelley, is it?'

'You are right,' said Bernard and, as Madeleine smiled, continued, 'It isn't Shelley.'

A tiny grimace of annoyance tugged at her mouth. 'Give me a clue.'

'Hmm. What clue can I give you? I'll tell you this—the author is not famous for anything else except that one line.'

'Oh, thank you. That's *really* helpful.' Madeleine looked at him hopefully, but Bernard didn't volunteer a second clue. 'No, I'm sorry. It's just one of those things I don't know. I'm never going to get it. You'd better tell me.'

Bernard smiled with a degree of complacency. 'The line comes from a poem called "Petra". . . .'

'I could have guessed that.'

'It was written by a gentleman who was born in 1813 and died in 1888. . . . He was a clergyman. . . .'

'Oh, do get on with it. I don't know the answer. You can just tell me,' Madeleine's voice was edged with petulance.

He looked up at her, an expression of surprised irritation on his face. It was a moment of conflict, the first snag in an evening that had up to that point been going perfectly.

Madeleine saw the danger and defused it by taking his hand in her gloved one, shaking it gently and saying in a little voice, 'Please tell me.'

Bernard's good humour was instantly restored. The lines around his brown eyes crinkled as he said. 'It was the Reverend John William Burgon.'

'Well, fancy that.' Her tone was ironic.

'Exactly. Totally unheard of, except for the one line.'

'Ah well,' said Madeleine casually, 'that's like:

One crowded hour of glorious life
Is worth an age without a name'

'Yes,' Bernard agreed, and, to Madeleine's vexation, identified the author: 'Thomas Osbert Mordaunt.'

For a moment she wondered if the weekend was a good idea. Was Bernard Hopkins really the right man, was he the one in the world who deserved Madeleine Severn? But, as she looked into his melancholy brown eyes, she knew it was right. They were in love, she was going to give herself to him completely, surrender her body to the gentleness of his experience. 'I'm so glad to be here with you,' she murmured.

His voice was almost inaudible with emotion as he responded, 'And I with you.'

Madeleine let go of his hand and picked up her champagne glass. She raised it in a toast, 'To us, Bernard. And to our love.'

The logs on the fire had disintegrated to deep red and the glow winked through the champagne as their glasses clinked together. The brown eyes gazed into the eyes which, so long ago, John Kaczmarek had described as 'forget-me-not wedded to violet'.

They were dilatory about tidying up the table and stacking the dishwasher. Partly it was because they were both self-consciously relaxing, desperate to show that they were in no hurry. But also in both of them there fluttered a little pulse of fear. Bernard grew more and more silent as time went on and eventually, after she had sponged down the kitchen surfaces sufficiently to meet even Mrs Rankin's high standards, it was Madeleine who asked, too breezily, 'Well, shall we go upstairs?'

Bernard nodded.

Except for a brief kiss on his arrival and the hand-holding over dinner, they had not touched each other in the course of the evening.

The bedroom seemed very small with the two of them in it. They loomed over the bed, filling all the available space. Madeleine stood irresolute. She wasn't quite sure what should happen next. She was waiting for a lead from Bernard. Would he take her in his arms and undress her, or was she expected to get ready for bed on her own?

Bernard seemed equally irresolute, so, before the silence became embarrassingly extended, Madeleine asked, 'Shall I use the bathroom first?'

Bernard, who had hardly spoken since the end of the meal, nodded.

She picked up her sponge-bag, her dressing gown and the new nightdress, and went through the low door into the bathroom. She took off her gloves and wondered for a moment what to do about her lenses. Under normal circumstances she would have taken them out at this stage in the evening, but she wasn't quite sure of the correct procedure on such a special occasion. How much should one be able to *see* when losing one's virginity? She made her decision and took the lenses out. After that she undressed and washed carefully. She had contemplated having a bath to relax her, but she did not want to keep Bernard waiting too long. Anyway, it was only a few hours since she had had one.

She looked at her body in the small mirror and was pleased with what she saw. True, it was no longer a girl's body, but it had retained much of its tension. She couldn't help comparing the tightness of her breasts favourably with the stretched sagging of her sister's. She checked the smoothness of her armpits, though she had only shaved them that afternoon, and pulled the new nightdress over her head. She buttoned the pleated front up to her neck. Then, turning on both taps in the sink to disguise any unromantic sounds, she used the lavatory. Another brisk brushing of the red-gold hair, a couple more puffs of the perfume-spray, dressing-gown draped loosely over her shoulders, and Madeleine Severn was ready to meet her lover.

It was then that she noticed her hands. The cracks seemed to have widened even since before dinner. She put on some more of the cream and rubbed the hands together as if washing them, but they still looked raw and ugly. It was maddening. Otherwise she knew she was looking so good, and yet suddenly she was handicapped by this disfigurement.

There was nothing else for it. She put her long gloves back on again. The effect in the mirror was perhaps eccentric, but not unattractive.

She lifted the latch, bowed beneath the low doorway and went into the bedroom.

Bernard was sitting on the bed. He was turned away from her.

'Bathroom's free,' she said, once more too breezily.

He rose from the bed, picked up a small overnight case and, still without looking at Madeleine, went through the low door to the bathroom.

Madeleine lay in bed, on the right side, affecting to read, holding the book very close to her unlensed eyes, tensely aware of every creak and gurgle that came from the bathroom. On the table at her side was her crammed brief-case. She had looked at her reading-matter and decided that *The Poems of Emily Dickinson* best fitted the occasion. She flicked through, but, though her eyes followed the familiar lines, her mind kept sliding off them. She had opened the book at the 'Love' section, usually an unfailing source of pleasure, but the only verse that held her attention was this:

Come slowly, Eden!
Lips unused to thee,
Bashful, sip thy jasmines,
As the fainting bee,

281

Reaching late his flower,
Round her chamber hums,
Counts his nectars—enters,
And is lost in balms!

The poem calmed her. Its mention of jasmines was serendipitous in the setting of Winter Jasmine Cottage. As ever for Madeleine, literature had the power to take the sharp edge off reality.

The door from the bathroom clicked open, and Bernard came in. He held the small case in his left hand; in his right were his shoes, and over his right arm his clothes were neatly folded. He wore light green pyjamas with dark green collar and cuffs. He kept his eyes and his body averted from Madeleine and the bed while he laid his clothes over a chair.

Madeleine concentrated on her book as she felt the mattress give to take his weight. He pulled the bedclothes over himself and lay back on the pillow. There was a silence.

'Emily Dickinson, eh?' His voice was deep and very close beside her.

'Yes. Yes, it is,' she replied fatuously.

'Brought your brief-case with you, I see,'

he said, trying without complete success to lighten his voice. 'Reckoning to catch up on work over the weekend, are you?'

'Oh no, not that.' She sat up now, needing to be busy, needing to occupy her hands, needing to end the embarrassment of his proximity. She pointed out the contents of her bag as she itemised them. 'It's just that I put so much stuff in here that I never like to be without it. You know, books, newspapers, addresses, theatre programmes, prints. . . . It's just me, I'm afraid. This bag is like me, really, mind full of all kinds of things, you know, a bit scatty. . . .' She was gabbling. There didn't seem to be enough objects in the bag to keep her going. She needed to keep talking; she needed to re-establish their intellectual empathy before the physical encounter. 'And all kinds of bits and pieces slip down to the bottom . . . pens and pencils . . . and, oh, there's my stapler. I've been looking for that for weeks. And that's a hair-slide . . . and a catalogue from an art exhibition and—'

She stopped dead.

'Why on earth do you carry that?' asked Bernard, looking at the black-handled sheath-knife.

'Well, I. . . . To be quite honest I'd forgotten it was there. I confiscated it from one of my students. I mean, really, you can't have them coming in to tutorials armed to the teeth?' She let out a little giggle. 'Can you?'

'No,' Bernard's voice sounded abstracted. He looked hard at the knife.

'Still, don't want that.' Madeleine's gloved hand put it down firmly on the bedside-table. 'Or this.' She put *The Poems of Emily Dickinson* down beside the knife, and turned to face Bernard. 'Hello,' she said softly.

'Hello,' he echoed and, awkwardly, put his arms around her.

For a moment they lay wordless and still.

'It's warm,' said Madeleine. Her tensions were easing. This was quite cosy, being held in the warmth of the bed. It was reminiscent of childhood. It was just a cuddle, nothing frightening.

Bernard kept a space between their bodies. He too felt calmed. There was nothing to be afraid of. With a woman whom he loved, it would be different. His erection was hard and firm. It was all quite natural. He was with a woman to whom he wanted to make love, and he would make love to her. All the confusions in his mind would resolve themselves. At last he would be normal.

He moved his face towards hers and kissed her. At first their lips just touched dryly and drew back. Then they touched for longer, then they were pressing each other apart, then liquid, turning, tongues joining. Bernard felt the moist opening and giving of her lips, and desperately needed the other opening and giving that they parallelled. His arms closed behind her back and pressed the softness of her body against the hardness of his own.

The need in him was now furiously urgent, the need that had gone unsatisfied for over thirty years. He rolled his body over on top of hers, disengaging his hands which came round to knead and pummel her breasts through the crisp pleats of the nightdress. The lower part of his body was thrusting through the fabric at the tight knot of her legs. His hands reached down in desperation, first to pull off his pyjamas, then scrabbling to raise the white skirt and give him access.

This was not how Madeleine had envisaged it. The cuddling had been nice, the gentle exploratory kissing had been nice. She had felt herself slowly aroused, felt a melting within as he touched her. But this sudden animal attack was different. There was no beauty in this, no romance in the jabbing and ransacking of her privacy. It was too fast, too fierce; it was not the gentle rhythm that her own fingers could so regularly find. Her gloved hands were no longer around him, pulling him towards her; now they were pushing, trying to hold him off, trying to force away the urgent sweatiness of his flesh. 'No, no,' she shouted. 'No. Not like this.'

'I know what I'm doing.' He almost spat the words at her, and closed her mouth with a kiss. But this was not a gentle kiss, it was like a gag to silence her, to stifle her perhaps. There was no tenderness; his teeth were hard and bruising on her lips.

His hands had now fought away the skirts of the white nightdress and were reaching, scratching, digging into the privacy between her rigid legs. Madeleine tried to scream, but his mouth was still clamped on hers, stopping her breath. She tried to scratch and pinch his chest, but through the gloves her nails had no power to hurt.

Suddenly she felt the body above her twitch and shudder. Bernard detached his mouth from hers and let out a little whimper of despair. Then, odiously, Madeleine felt a viscous warmth spreading across the private flesh below her navel.

The weight of Bernard's body was suddenly lifted off and he threw himself to the far side of the bed, with his back to her.

'Well, really!' Madeleine burst out, when she had sufficient breath for indignation. 'What on earth did you think you were doing?'

'I know what I'm doing,' Bernard's voice was petulantly dogged, but edged with despair.

'No, you don't. God, if that was meant to be making love. . . . That had nothing to do with love.'

'If you'd been more gentle, if you had been more loving, it would have been all right.' His tone was now one of whining adolescence.

'Huh. Why should I be gentle, when you behave like an animal? God,' she said with sudden venom, 'you revolt me!'

Suddenly he was once more facing her, his hands tight and pinching on her shoulders, his eyes only inches from hers. 'Revolt you?'

'Yes,' she hissed. 'You're disgusting and pathetic. And,' she added viciously, 'you can't even do it properly.'

There did not seem to have been time for him to move, before she felt the immobilising weight of his body on top of her and the pressure of his rigid fingers on her throat.

Desperately she reached her gloved hand round for the black-handled sheath-knife on the table.

But Bernard saw what she was doing, and their two hands reached for the weapon together.

PART THREE

After The Murder

23

During the Christmas rush, Tony Ashton helped out as a barman in Sharon's father's pub. After Christmas he stayed on. By the time he and Sharon announced their engagement the following May, Tony was managing two of the bars. (He had also by then been prevailed upon to abandon his ear-ring.) And by the time they were married, in the November of that year, Sharon had managed to get her fiancé to share her interests in mortgages, fitted kitchens and matching bathroom suites. Their first house was bought, decorated and ready to move into by the time that, on their wedding night, in a hotel in Paris, just like something out of one of her favourite romances, Sharon relinquished her virginity.

Paul Grigson confounded expectation by being accepted at Oxford. Perhaps some of Madeleine's coaching had paid off; or perhaps his brush with the police had concentrated his mind sufficiently for him to get the best out of his natural intelligence.

He had appeared in court on a considerable accumulation of charges after his adventure in Pulborough, but skilful legal representation had so convincingly attributed his behaviour to anxiety about his examinations and his mother's state of health that he got off lightly (although it would be some time before he could contemplate continuing his driving lessons).

Mrs Grigson got better. The hospital, after running every test they could think of on her, finally isolated a food allergy as the cause of her illness. By keeping strictly to the prescribed diet, she was able to return to a completely normal life.

She was delighted that her son had justified her confidence by getting to Oxford. (She even wrote a letter, thanking him for the school's help, to Julian Garrett, who added it to the file that he always produced to convince the wavering parents of potential pupils.) Her ambitions for Paul had been achieved and so she was not too reluctant to accede to her son's request to spend four months doing Voluntary Service in Nigeria.

The separation was good for both of them. After a few weeks in Africa, Paul lost his virginity to and had an eight-week affair with an uncomplicated German girl called Helga. The relationship only ended because of her return to Germany, but it was not continued. Both of them were keen to meet other people. Paul managed another brief sexual fling in Nigeria, had two more back in Brighton that summer, and looked forward to meeting the female undergraduates when he started at Oriel College in the autumn.

He hardly thought of Madeleine Severn after the last time that he saw her. Paul Grigson grew up.

The murderer continued to work at the Garrettway School of Languages as if nothing had happened.

After the tussle in the bed of Winter Jasmine Cottage when, with strength she did not know she possessed, Madeleine had snatched the knife from Bernard and stabbed him in the chest, she had gone very calm and worked out her escape-route. The nightdress, whose pleated front was soaked in blood, she had decided to leave. It was such a new purchase that no one could relate it to her. Taking it off and leaving it by the side of the bed, she had had a long, relaxing bath, then meticulously tidied up and removed every trace of herself from the cottage. She even picked a few red-gold strands from the pillow and checked for them by the dressing-table and in the bathroom where she had brushed her hair.

Before midnight she was in her Renault 5 and driving back to Brighton.

After the police had been summoned to Winter Jasmine Cottage the following Wednesday by Mrs Rankin, they started an exhaustive investigation into the murder. They questioned Bernard Hopkins' employer and colleagues at the Garrettway School of Languages. The hint from Stella Franklin of a possible romance between Bernard and Madeleine led them to question the latter in considerable detail and for a while their suspicions were strong.

They had, however, no evidence against her. The attack of eczema which had forced her to wear gloves meant that there were none of her fingerprints anywhere at Winter Jasmine Cottage. The remoteness of the location meant that no one had seen any arrivals or departures on the relevant night, and the frosty ground ruled out the possibility of her vehicle being identified by tyre-marks.

Besides, Madeleine had an unshakeable alibi. Her niece, Laura, could vouch for her having been in the Kemp Town house all of the weekend. They had stayed up late on the Friday night talking, risen early on the Saturday morning and spent all the rest of the time together. There was no way that Madeleine could have been in Pulborough at the time when the police experts were convinced the murder had taken place.

The one person who might have told a different story, Laura's boyfriend Terry (whose mother had died when he was a child and who went back to Worcester every weekend to his unsuspecting wife), was never going to break her alibi. No one had any reason to connect him with the house in Kemp Town, and that was the way he intended things should stay. Apart from anything else, he was getting a little bored with Laura's unquestioning devotion and had decided the relationship wasn't going to go the distance. So when, a fortnight after the murder, his work in Brighton ended, he did not bother to call her again. (And when, a month later, Laura found herself to be pregnant and, not wishing to repeat Aggie's mistake, arranged an abortion, Terry never knew anything about it. Nor did Laura's mother. Nor did her aunt.)

The other person who might have threatened Madeleine was Julian Garrett. He had, after all, seen her on the night of the murder, in the Garrettway School of Languages at a very unusual time and apparently in disguise. But Julian's attitude to responsibility pervaded all aspects of his life. The idea that Madeleine might have murdered Bernard gave him a little ironic amusement, but he was never going to volunteer information that might link her with the crime. Leave well enough alone, thought Julian, as usual, and looked forward to the spring, when he would be able to bring a little romance into the lives of the new influx of nubile foreigners.

The police investigation into Madeleine might have gone deeper, if they had not suddenly received new information from the Metropolitan Police linking Bernard Hopkins with a series of prostitute killings which had been going on over the previous five years. The manner of 'Mandy's' murder closely echoed the other cases; samples of semen and saliva matched. So the enquiry went off in a completely different direction and the police moved towards the conclusion that the murderer was yet another prostitute whom Bernard had enticed down to a country cottage and who had turned the tables on him. Though questioning around the London underworld, particularly of friends of former victims, led nowhere, the new approach to the investigation had the effect of taking the heat off Madeleine. She even, later, received a letter of apology from the police for the pressure of questioning that she had undergone.

So Madeleine Severn continued her life unchanged. Her virginity, like that of Bernard Hopkins, remained intact to the end of her life.

Paul Grigson moved on. Tony and Sharon Ashton moved on. But Madeleine Severn, who had not really changed since her university days, remained the same. She dressed the same, she listened to the same music, she read the same poetry, she taught the same tutorials based on the same Oxford essays. She told people the same romantic derivation of her surname, about her descent from the Joseph Severn who had accompanied Keats on his last journey to Italy (conveniently forgetting that she had been the first to drop the 'i' from the family name of Severin).

She continued to patronise her sister, though she did not get the opportunity to do the same to her niece, who moved away from Brighton after the abortion and never contacted her aunt again. Madeleine continued to inspire occasional crushes among her more impressionable students and, when questioned in quiet moments, would admit to the great sadness of her life, her perfect romance with a young man called John Kaczmarek, who unfortunately had died.

As she grew older, Madeleine Severn's mannerisms became eccentricities, but she was unaware of the change. Though she might hear people sniggering, it never occurred to her that she was the object of their amusement. Her sense of well-being, like her virginity, remained intact.

And, when, very occasionally, images of a night spent at Winter Jasmine Cottage,

Shorton, near Pulborough, flashed into her mind, she was able swiftly to dispel them. Some things she preferred not to think about.

The publishers hope that this
Large Print Book has brought
you pleasurable reading.
Each title is designed to make
the text as easy to see as possible.
G.K. Hall Large Print Books
are available from your library and
your local bookstore. Or you can
receive information by mail on
upcoming and current Large Print Books
and order directly from the publishers.
Just send your name and address to:

G.K. Hall & Co.
70 Lincoln Street
Boston, Mass. 02111

or call, toll-free:

1-800-343-2806

A note on the text
Large print edition designed by
Bernadette Montalvo.
Composed in 16 pt. Plantin
on a Xyvision 300/Linotron 202N
by Genevieve Connell
of G.K. Hall & Co.